SHE NEEDS

NEXT DOOR ROMANCE

LLE LOVE

MY ROMANCE

CONTENTS

About the Author	v
Sign Up to Receive Free Books	vii
Blurb	ix
1. Chapter 1	1
2. Chapter 2	12
3. Chapter 3	27
4. Chapter 4	37
5. Chapter 5	47
6. Chpater 6	53
7. Chapter 7	60
8. Chapter 8	72
9. Chapter 9	79
10. Chapter 10	90
11. Chapter 11	92
Sign Up to Receive Free Books	95
Preview of The Mountain Man's Secret	97
Chapter 1	99
Chapter 2	105
Chapter 3	109
Chapter 4	115
Other Books By This Author	122
About the Author	125

Made in "The United States" by:

Michelle Love

© Copyright 2020 – Michelle Love

ISBN: 978-1-64808-124-8

ALL RIGHTS RESERVED. No part of this publication may be reproduced or transmitted in any form whatsoever, electronic, or mechanical, including photocopying, recording, or by any informational storage or retrieval system without express written, dated and signed permission from the author

❦ Created with Vellum

ABOUT THE AUTHOR

Mrs. Love writes about smart, sexy women and the hot alpha billionaires who love them. She has found her own happily ever after with her dream husband and adorable 6 and 2 year old kids.
Currently, Michelle is hard at work on the next book in the series, and trying to stay off the Internet.
"Thank you for supporting an indie author. Anything you can do, whether it be writing a review, or even simply telling a fellow reader that you enjoyed this. Thanks

facebook.com/HotAndSteamyRomance

instagram.com/michellesromance

SIGN UP TO RECEIVE FREE BOOKS

Sign Up to Receive Free E-Books and Audiobook Codes.

Would you like to read **The Unexpected Nanny, Dirty Little Virgin** and **other romance books** for **free**?

You can sign up to receive these free e-books and audiobooks by typing this link into your browser:

https://www.steamyromance.info/free-books-and-audiobooks-hot-and-steamy/

Or this one:

https://www.steamyromance.info/the-unexpected-nanny-free/

BLURB

He's the only man I've ever wanted

He's my superhero.
Tall, dark, and handsome, Damon Case has it all: wealth, power, a mysterious past, and the body of a God.
He protects the town, and he's protected me, forcing my awful parents to stop hurting me.
I don't care how checkered his past is. I have to have him.
He tells me I'm too good for him.
But without him, I'm lost; he's the only man who can make me feel safe.

Now suddenly, criminals have come to our small town, and I'm one of their targets.
And here comes Damon to my rescue again.
I finally get my one night in his arms, but dawn brings a terrible revelation.
One of the boys who attacked me has been shot dead, and Damon's the prime suspect.

**Damon swore he would never kill again...
But if he didn't pull the trigger, who did?**

Damon: Sweet little Amy's all grown up now, and she tempts me every time I see her...

She was the little girl I took home when she got left behind at the market and the teenager I helped when her parents locked her out.
Now, she's grown into the most amazing, sweet, sexy woman I have ever met.
I can't find satisfaction with any other woman in bed unless I think of Amy—angel-faced Amy who thinks I'm a hero.
When a leg injury sends her home from college for a semester, she's back in my territory.
She's more beautiful, sweet, and understanding than ever.
I shouldn't stain her with my bloody hands...but God, do I want to.

Now some of the boys in my town have gone bad, and they've targeted my Amy.
I'll do anything to protect her—except kill again. I promised.
But the very night I finally have her in my arms, one of the boys turns up murdered.
She thinks I did it. And now she's fled.

**That hot little gem of a girl loves me in spite of my past...
I've got to clear my name for her no matter what it takes.**

CHAPTER 1

Amy

My blood burns with frustration as I run. My running shoes slap the sidewalk beneath me with every step. I'm just not getting better fast enough. I'm not even back to half my normal speed, and I can feel the ache in my underused muscles after only a few blocks.

I DON'T WANT to overdo exercising. My physical therapist, Mike, has already warned me about what can happen if I do. I have only had the cast off for a few weeks; I should only be doing this at a walking pace, just like I do after breakfast every day.

BUT RIGHT NOW I am so pissed off at Mom and Dad that I have to burn off my anger somehow before I go back home.

"Amy, I know you're still healing, but you need to go back to the

dorms as soon as summer is over. Your dad and I like the peace and quiet, honey. We're paying for you to live on campus as much for our convenience as yours.

"You're twenty. You can't expect us to put you up forever."

Bitch. The thought makes me feel a little guilty. It's not that I don't understand where Mom is coming from—the two-bedroom bungalow where I grew up just isn't big enough for three adults.

But I'm sick to death of being reminded over and over again of what a sacrifice they're making by taking me in. I'm their daughter and I've been injured. It's not like I'm some random moocher off the street. They've never been the best at parenting, but Mom's really being selfish about this.

I manage to make it to the top of the first hill before stopping to rest my leg and catch my breath. How many months of training have I lost thanks to that stupid kid, his stupid inattentive parents, and that stupid tree well? *It was a skiing accident, Mom, not a bid to inconvenience you.*

She'd actually had the nerve to shed a few tears when I said it. And then she turned around and went right back to acting like my shattered leg was exactly that—an inconvenience.

. . .

I'D BE LESS pissed about Mom and Dad wanting to get rid of me if they would just be fair about it. I hadn't asked for some unattended little boy to blunder suddenly into my path in the middle of a damn black diamond slope. I definitely hadn't asked to be sent veering into a tree to avoid him.

I WAS BOTH REALLY lucky and really unlucky in those desperate seconds after dodging the kid. I'd slowed down enough on that steep slope to keep from killing myself, but then the snow at the foot of a tree crumbled under me, and I dropped into darkness. I don't remember a damn thing after that until I woke up in the hospital.

MY SHATTERED LEG cost me an entire semester of school. I spent all spring moping around in a cast between sessions with Mike and arguments with my parents; I'm eager to get back to Denver. But on that day when I was wheeled out of the hospital, the last thing I needed was grief about having to depend on Mom and Dad for a while.

BUT THAT DOESN'T MATTER to them. My mother's "just being honest" nagging started right after I told her that Dr. Lenz hadn't cleared me to return to school for the summer semester. She was really mad about that—mad at me.

I ASKED her what she expected me to do, and she waved her arms and went on about how she didn't know; she was just expressing her feelings. Meanwhile Dad, as quietly remote as Mom is dramatic, hid behind his newspaper. Yet I have no doubt that he's the one that will change the locks as soon as my car pulls away from the curb.

After Mom's stupid lecture, I had to leave for a while. And this first attempt at a beloved night run is helping my blood cool down.

The town of Jagged Butte is small and sleepy enough that most of the time, night runs aren't a problem so long as the weather allows them. The crime rate is so low that we have only one guy handling local law enforcement, and he's a county deputy, not a full sheriff—but for a population of five thousand, it's surprisingly enough.

My hometown sprawls across the broken-looking top of the butte whose name it bears, high up enough that you need strong lungs to live here. Everything branches off of a single main street that meanders up from the interstate and runs from hill to hill. There's one school complex, one library, two food stores, one clinic, one movie theater, a few other shops, and five bed and breakfasts to accommodate the winter skiers and summer hikers.

People here are divided into two types: the ones with real money and land who live back in the woods, and the rest of us who live and work in town. Some folks come in from the surrounding villages and hamlets to swell the population during the day, and of course, there are the tourists. But mostly it's us—the Townies—who populate the town with occasional visits from our rich, aloof neighbors when they need to stock up on supplies.

As I jog along, I have a better view of the big houses scattered through the hills than during the day; their twinkling lights give them away from behind their screen of trees. Some of those estates cover more land than the town itself. Others are no more than a nice house and yard on half an acre of space. And then there's Damon's Tower.

I look up at the mountainside where I can see it in clear weather: a tall, black shadow against the sky, rising from the forested slope, its silhouette pierced with bits of light. Tonight, it's clear enough that I can see the shining windows, the driveway lights snaking up to its base, and further back, a faint twinkle of fairy lights in the garden.

I've never visited that place—except in my dreams. But the man who lives there...Damon...just thinking about him makes my anger dissipate faster than a run could ever fix.

My heart lifts and I start running again, feeling fresh energy fill my stride. Maybe I'll actually get to see him tonight. If he's in town, then he'll be out watching over us.

Damon Case is the guardian of the Butte, plain and simple. Not only does he own almost half the real estate here, but he takes responsibility for day-to-day comforts too.

. . .

If your heat gets shut off, he makes one phone call and it's restored. If you crash your car, he'll send a tow. People rarely ask him to do anything for them except when they're really desperate. But when it comes to baseline survival, we Townies are covered.

And that's just the above-board stuff that he does for us. Damon has a secret—only it's not a secret from me. And it makes him even more heroic in my eyes—and even more irresistible.

I speed up a little as I think about him. Knowing that Damon secretly patrols the town at night is the reason I started my nighttime runs. I always went out hoping I would run into our local protector by chance.

Sometimes it worked. Sometimes we talked. And once, we almost did more.

Hi, remember me? I'm Amy Gatlin, the girl who's had a crush on you since I hit puberty? I'm here with a bum leg and a kiss...I've been saving the kiss for you.

The Guardian, as some of the Townie kids have taken to calling him, has always been in my life. He's always been the only one to make me feel safe, and I've loved him in different ways my whole life. At first, I wished he would rescue me and be my dad instead of the wordless creep at my breakfast table. Then, I wished he would rescue me and train me to be a badass like him.

THEN MY HORMONES KICKED IN—AND things got a little more complicated. Deliciously complicated. My days were filled with breathless fantasies that followed me into my dreams at night. But from the beginning, long before I wanted him to be my lover, Damon Case was my hero.

WHEN MY MOTHER "ABSENTMINDEDLY" left me at the store at age six, Damon was the one who drove me home, handed me tissues for my tears, and told me that she shouldn't have done that. When she did it again when I was seven years old, then again at seven and a half, eight…he simply showed up with his car and drove me home. And perhaps best of all, he'd knock hard on the door once we got there.

WHEN SHE OPENED IT, he would look her straight in the eye and demand an explanation, and she would flutter and cry and babble about how stressful parenting was and how she promised that she would do better. My father, a cowardly little weasel of a man, would sit mute in his chair and glare at Damon sullenly like a kid being lectured after getting in trouble.

DAD SEEMS to resent Damon even now. But they're both afraid of him. I'm certain that fear may have saved my life once.

. . .

When I came home ten minutes late from a winter party at age sixteen, my house keys mysteriously missing, I discovered that my Dad had "accidentally" locked me out in twenty degree temps; it was Damon Case that I called. He stood there with me knocking on the door until my mother finally answered. I still remember her, poised to yell at me but freezing in her tracks, horrified to see the tall, black-haired man standing beside me yet again on the chilly porch.

I remember staring at my parents' paling faces as he said coldly in his faint Oxford accent, "I have quite a thick file on your attempts to abandon your daughter. You have been warned multiple times."

He loomed over my tiny, cold-hearted father, arms folded. "Deliberately locking her out for the night in below-freezing weather is attempted murder. Did you steal her house key from her bag to make it more convenient for you, Mr. Gatlin?"

My father started shaking, sweat beading on his forehead, as he dug in his pants pocket to produce my key, saying absolutely nothing the whole time. It was only then that I realized that even though my mother might be a dramatic bitch, my father is an entirely new level of toxic.

Damon forced him to give me back my key and then calmly explained to them that they were going to behave themselves, leave me alone to get good grades, send me off to college, and never give him any reason to visit them again. They both nodded at him, eyes as big as dinner plates.

. . .

AND AFTER THAT, they did behave—and kept behaving—until I broke my leg.

BUT IT WAS that last cold, blustery evening that I fell in love with Damon Case for keeps. That night, I had truly wished that he would take me home with him, because I was tired of living with these hopeless, heartless parents. Instead, I dreamed of him every night, and during the day he was never far from my thoughts. And it's been that way ever since.

I DON'T WANT anyone else. No one measures up to him. No boy my own age, or anyone older or younger for that matter, has ever affected me in any way since that day.

JUST THE THOUGHT of that tall, powerfully-built figure in his dark coat, stepping in out of nowhere to fix things without asking anything in return, is enough to leave me lying awake horny as hell. He's one of the few things about the Butte that I missed when I was in Denver. And I haven't been out of the house enough over the last months to see if he's even still around.

MY PARENTS WALKED on eggshells for a solid month after Damon's final warning, and eventually things started to resemble a textbook version of normal. Things got a whole lot easier for me then. Despite the way they treated me my whole life, I gave them no real reason to give me any trouble. I was always a good kid, even if my mother's endless nitpicking and complaining might have led people to think otherwise.

. . .

Deep down, I think she knows it's wrong to treat me this way; she can find no reason to complain, so she fabricates them. In the end, I know she's just angry that she became a mother at all. And as for my father? He never talks enough for me to ever figure out why he's so mad at me.

Maybe he's been in a twenty-year sulk because the one child my mother agreed to produce didn't have a dick. Or maybe he just hates everyone. He's estranged from his whole family. Sometimes I think about looking them up hoping it might help me find out what the hell is wrong with him.

I need to stop thinking about all this bullshit, or I won't calm down enough to go home. I only have to last one more month, and then I can head back to school. Once I'm there, I'll have peace and quiet again, and I can work on getting back in shape. If I want, in just one more month, I can stop calling my parents all together: no more trying to make stilted conversation with them, no more forcing a relationship on them that they don't want.

They never call me on their own anyway, and that's fine with me. After dealing with my mother's emotional outbursts and my father's icy silence and quiet sabotage all these many years, I'm burned out. I'm starting to want their role in my life to be as tiny as their love for me.

Twenty-nine days until I leave for Denver. I know they'll pay for the winter semester and my dorm again just to keep me out of their hair. I'll take advantage of it. And if I come to visit the Butte this winter, it won't be to see them.

. . .

Though my childhood wasn't great, I know it could have been a lot worse. I had a roof over my head, food in my belly, medical care, and now college. But it still hurts.

I have to tough it out for now. One day I'll have the money to walk away for good. I'll find someone to love me and have a family of my own. And those two will never be a part of it. I'll never subject any children of mine to the cold treatment of my parents.

My eyes blur with tears as I start forward again picking up my pace. I ignore it. It's just the wind coming off the mountains.

Whenever I think of my future, I still hope that the lover that takes front and center would be the mysterious man in the Tower. But Damon's much older than I am—he has to be in his forties now. He saw me grow up. He might still think of me as a kid.

But he's still the man of my dreams. And I still hope, optimism slowly replacing my anger and grief, that I'll run into him again tonight...just like I used to.

CHAPTER 2

Damon

Amy Gatlin shouldn't be going out on runs yet. I've seen her X-rays and physical therapy reports: there's titanium in that leg now, scars that need to loosen, muscles to build up. What the hell is she doing?

SHE'S AT LEAST BEING a little sensible, stopping to rest and flex her leg experimentally, remembering to rehydrate from her water bottle—but it's still too soon. From my vantage point back in the trees, I watch her run through my night-vision goggles. I detect her slight limp that tells me she's pushing it a touch too hard.

SWEETHEART, don't do that. You know better. You want that limp to get worse?

I'm tempted to call the cell phone number she's kept all these years to tell her to take it easy. But if we get to talking again, I know what will happen. And it can't happen.

THAT DOESN'T KEEP me from staring. *God, she's blossomed even more since I saw her last.* Now that she's not all bruises and bandages in a hospital bed, she's the most beautiful woman in town.

HER HONEY-COLORED ponytail shines even in the dim streetlights as she jogs steadily down the hill. I remember her eyes being almost the exact same color as her hair and full of warmth. She's in plain blue track pants and a white tank top with a reflective belt and bracelets on to warn any oncoming cars. With every step she takes, a bear whistle around her neck bounces against her full breasts.

I COULD DRINK in the sight of her all night.

I'VE BEEN many things in my life. I've seen combat on three continents. I've been a killer. I'm a billionaire, and I'm the man in charge in Jagged Butte...and I've never had such a big problem. Her name is Amy, and she's young enough to be my daughter.

SHE'S like a wisteria vine cracking through the sidewalk from sheer will, persevering enough to grow, thrive, and flower. I've watched her struggle under the "care" of her neglectful parents;

I've watched her grieve and fight to win their approval; and I've watched her finally give up and leave for Denver. And I've missed her for those two years when I have no right to think about her at all.

She's young and innocent and clear-hearted and kind. All she ever seemed to want as a kid was to be loved and protected. I couldn't help but try and look after her.

But then she started looking at me like I'm some kind of Goddamn hero just for treating her like she deserves. And then...then she went and got a crush on me.

I still remember the day it happened. It had two effects on me that were pretty damn dangerous. First, it made me want to beat her father's ass. Her mother was—and is—a bitch, but she's all talk. Her father, the scheming little coward, says nothing, but then steals her keys and locks her out in the deadly cold.

Beat him? If I look really deeply into my feelings on the matter, I want to put a bullet in him. I've got no Goddamn objectivity when it comes to that girl.

That day Amy first looked at me with want in her eyes, I fell. Hard. Like I haven't in years.

. . .

That someone should look at *me* like that, after everything I've done in my life...well, it made me want to earn it.

It wasn't sexual at first. She was just a pretty sixteen year old—off limits, like everyone underage—but I became obsessed with protecting her and giving her someone to lean on.

But once she bloomed into a woman on me and got bold enough to start subtly flirting, it took everything I had to pretend to be oblivious. And I was *definitely* pretending.

Once she was grown, she gained more power over me than any woman ever has. One tiny, tender smile from her was as good as a hand stroking my cock to attention. But eighteen or not, I still had to fight my feelings.

And if we talk again, I know I will struggle. I don't deserve someone as pure and sweet as her, no matter how much my body might try to tell me otherwise.

I'm tainted. My hands are bloodied, and I'm twice her damn age. I can't make her happy, and I know it. So I've worked very hard to push aside my feelings for her and to ignore how much I've missed seeing her lovely face around town.

It never works. When I heard she was hurt, I flew to her side as fast as I could without everyone finding out. I pray she has no idea that I was there; I'd have a hard time explaining it.

I PAID HER MEDICAL BILLS, too, knowing that her parents would argue against their responsibility to pay them even if she is on their insurance. I never revealed that I was paying for Amy's care. I'm sure her folks just let the hospital bills pile up, never opening any to discover only receipts.

Very expensive receipts. If it wasn't for me making sure she received the best care, no matter the cost, Amy might have lost the damn leg. Her parents literally didn't give a damn.

WHY THE FUCK didn't they just put her up for adoption? Was her mother just keeping her as a way of blackmailing Gatlin into staying in the damn marriage? God, the old me would have shot them both without even thinking about it.

AMY'S PARENTS are horrible people. I hope Amy has built herself a support system back in Denver with people who treat her far better. I also hope that she has a boyfriend back in Denver now —a good one, who gives her all the love she deserves.

BECAUSE IF NOT, I know she's got another reason other than recovery to be out running around tonight: me. And that can't start up again. Not that anything ever happened, but...I know how close things got.

. . .

AMY HAD all kinds of excuses for starting her nightly runs. I had all kinds of excuses to be waiting for her at this particular lookout. Then she made up other excuses to start finding me and to bring me a thermos of coffee every night.

I MADE up excuses to interrupt my watch, so I could indulge in that coffee and talk. We made excuses to get to know each other. To befriend each other.

I DIDN'T TELL her about my past, of course—or why I thoroughly didn't deserve it when, that last night before she left for college, we almost kissed.

SHE WAS IN MY ARMS. I was wiping her tears away. She was recovering from the latest spat of grief over some new garbage her parents were putting her through.

I WAS TELLING her that the fault lay entirely with them just as I always did. I told her that she didn't deserve any of this—that they were just crappy parents. I was trying not to notice the curves of her strong, lush young body as she pressed against me. I was praying she didn't notice how, now that she was grown, she could coax my cock painfully awake with a simple embrace.

BUT EITHER SHE noticed or she was so overwhelmed by the moment, because she cupped my face and gazed up at me with trust and desire. Those lush lips had parted invitingly, and I almost bent to them. It had hurt to pull away, apologize, and endure her disappointment.

That near miss has haunted my dreams ever since. It has also fucked up my sex life. No matter how hard I try, no matter how hot the woman, I can't finish when I'm fucking anyone unless I imagine it's sweet, barely-legal Amy who's trembling under me.

Once I do though, I blast off—harder than I ever have. I swear to God, that girl has become my fetish.

If I'd kissed her that night, I would have fucked her that night, as inevitably as the Goddamn tide. We both wanted it, but I forced myself to hold off. I'm not sure I would have the strength to do it again.

But now here she is, running at night again, and here I am, pausing in my patrol of the town so that I can watch her. Heart beating fast, dick hard as marble, I know that I'm in trouble...again.

She is starting to limp, just slightly. The sight makes me tense. Pretty, limping young women isolated on dark streets draw predators like flies in the big city.

However, the Butte is anything but big, and aside from passive-aggressive pieces of crap like Amy's parents, there aren't very many predators here. But all it takes is one. So I keep my eye on her and try to ignore my growing desire as I watch.

I'VE BEEN PATROLLING these streets for almost as long as Amy has been alive. It started after I moved back home. After the vast, black, and deadly nights of Afghanistan, Somalia, and Thailand, the peace I found in my home town was too complete; its nights too cozy.

I DIDN'T TRUST IT. So I went out to check for trouble that first night I was home. I did a patrol of the town around midnight, laid down to sleep for a few hours, woke up from the nightmares, and patrolled it again just before dawn.

I'VE BEEN DOING it nightly ever since whenever I'm in town. Once I know everyone up here is safe, I can rest easy. But not before.

I'M SURE LOVELY, adoring Amy figured out my pattern. She's incredibly smart—way smarter than her parents give her credit for. The coffee she brought would be so fresh that I knew she was timing me.

I MISS THOSE NIGHTS. I miss her. Part of me hopes we'll run into each other. Every part of me but my damn, nagging conscience, actually.

I DON'T KNOW if I can deal with a midnight meeting. She's twenty and even more beautiful and sexy than before. My list of excuses for not ending up in bed with her is getting shorter and shorter.

She always seemed so sweetly oblivious to all the signs that I was—and still am—laboring under a guilty conscience. She called me a hero once—and I was quick to correct her. But she doesn't know that I have my reasons beyond simple humility for rejecting that title coming from her innocent lips.

Heroes don't kill.

I only told her I was a soldier once. She doesn't know that I patrol, and help people, and save people, not out of benevolence, but out of guilt—and so I can fucking sleep. I know her crush would wither pretty damned quickly if she could see the blood on my hands.

Still, I have to admit that her belief in me, misguided or not, helps keep me going. I'm not a hero—but when she looks at me in her way, I want to be one. I spend a lot of time trying to live up to her expectations; in fact, over time, they have become my own as penance for my past.

Most of the people I've helped have all been in the same basic situations: accident, misadventure, too drunk to get home, too poor to cover essential bills. It's pretty easy to save and protect people from mundane crap like that. But now and again, a real problem comes to the Butte.

. . .

ONE OF THE EARLY YEARS, it was a serial killer. Wanted for murder in Denver, he was sniffing around for a fresh victim somewhere remote where he could get his sick thrills, then move on before any investigation really got rolling. The current deputy along with backup from a neighboring town caught him trying to break into a teenage girl's bedroom, thanks to a timely phone call from me.

NOBODY besides her and her family ever knew that I was waiting inside that bedroom with a gun, making sure that fucker never got close to her. Grateful for my protection, that family thinks I'm a hero too. They'll never know how close I came to just plugging the bastard and dropping him off a cliff before he even got into their yard.

ANOTHER TIME, one of our locals went through a bad divorce, snapped a little, and started setting fires. That time, I really lost my temper. After an anonymous tip, Deputy Metcalf found our arsonist locked inside a garage he had set on fire, battered and terrified, as the building smoldered around him.

THE ARSONIST never fingered me as the one who beat him and locked him in. He didn't dare. He moved out of town and never set another fire.

NOW, two of the shittiest parents in the Butte's history are driving Amy out of her home late in the evening. I know it's their fault she's pushing herself like this, because I caught the tears on her cheeks when she passed under a streetlight. It's clear she's badly distracted—and thus vulnerable.

It wouldn't worry me so much if not for her injury—and what happened two hours ago.

A bunch of local kids just came piling back into town for the summer last week. Now, they're cooped up, bored, horny, and too used to city life and free-flowing alcohol to keep still. Metcalf keeps picking them up and tossing them in jail for drunk and disorderly, reckless driving, open containers...and of course, harassing women.

I can't abide that crap, but it's the typical shit young men get into, and it's usually beneath my notice. Problem is, it seems to be escalating. Earlier tonight, I watched four of them teeter perilously close to dragging a terrified girl into their van.

That's why I'm not sure that Amy is safe out here alone. It's one more reason that I feel compelled to watch her. She's tough, but she's not up to speed on what's going on—and there are four of the bastards.

I should call her and warn her, but I'm not sure which would be more dangerous: letting her finish her run without knowing or the sparks that will fly if Amy and I get close to each other again. The risk that she'll run into them between here and home in a sprawling town of five thousand is pretty minimal, after all.

. . .

THE RISK that I will end up with Amy in my bed, that she'll fall even further in love, and that I'll lose all reason and refuse to let her go is one hundred percent. And if that happens, she'll learn the truth about me. Once it's out, she'll leave in horror, fucking destroying me in the process. The most terrible part of all is, if it wouldn't hurt her, it would almost be worth it.

I HAVE to get on with my work. Those boys are still around. I don't know what they're up to, but it can't be anything good. They could just as easily be targeting someone else tonight.

I CAN SEE HALF the town from my vantage point, but there's another half on the other side of the hill that also needs patrolling. I can't just watch over Amy, as lovely an idea as that is. Everyone deserves to be safe.

EXCEPT, of course, for the little shits who were hassling the Allen girl. I wasn't even patrolling when I caught them; I was headed down off the hill to the gas station to fuel up. Good thing I'm always paying attention.

THERE'S a certain body language that young girls have when boys or men are making them uncomfortable, and they struggle to be polite. Girls tend to be raised to be reasonable, to negotiate, to have manners. Boys...sometimes aren't. And predators take advantage of girls' misguided politeness.

THESE BOYS WERE ABOUT AS civilized as young hyenas. I didn't like watching them surround her and edge her closer to their open van door while she ducked her head and fussed nervously with her hair. I started walking over, and quickly got close enough to hear her pleading with them.

"I REALLY NEED to get home...I have a boyfriend...please don't touch me...no, I need you to let me go..."

IN THAT MOMENT, my blood started boiling, and I felt the weight of the pistol against the small of my back like a big, blue steel temptation. I've been through too many wars, both open and secret; I've killed too many men. I've worked hard to get rid of my killer instincts over the years, but it's difficult for me sometimes to look at some piece of human filth and not think that a bullet's the only cure.

IT MUST HAVE SHOWN in my face, because when one of the boys spied me, he stiffened in fear. I caught a brief flash of terrified blue eyes, and then he muttered something. They all suddenly scrambled for the van's shelter like a nest of disturbed rats, leaving the confused but relieved teen girl standing alone.

THE VAN SCREECHED AWAY as I ran up.

THE BOYS WERE all dressed in blue jeans, new trainers in bright colors, and white hoodies that they had pulled tight around their faces. Even under the light from the streetlamp, I hadn't been able to pick out their identities, and I noticed they had ripped off the van's license plate as well.

I DON'T KNOW who they are or where to find them. And that pisses me off as much as their behavior.

I DROVE THE GIRL, whose first name was Cassie, back home along with two other girls, and got as much information from them as I could without upsetting them. Cassie was fifteen and lived just up the road; she and her friends had been going for snacks mid-movie marathon. She had headed to the restroom on the backside of the gas station and found herself surrounded by the boys.

SHE HAD no idea who they were either. None of the girls did; the other two, Molly and Kate, were shocked to find out what Cassie had endured. I have no way of tracking those little scumbags in real time on so little information, so I have to keep watch and wait for them to pop up again.

I CAN'T DO that from here. Amy will finish her run soon and then she'll be safely indoors. Meanwhile, those boys could be stalking someone else. I need to move my ass.

I GET up from my blind—a stand of dense bushes with a camouflage screen behind it—and head over to pull the camouflage drape off my Jeep. It's one of my usual lookouts—and it used to be where Amy would find me, bringing her sweet smile and a thermos of good coffee. She's slowly headed this way now, maybe hoping she'll run into me.

I NEED to stop waiting for her and get moving. The town needs me. Lovely, perfect Amy does not—no matter how much she still believes she does.

CHAPTER 3

Amy

My leg is starting to hurt by the time I reach the thick stand of bushes that I know doubles as one of Damon's lookout posts. I sigh, glad at least that I've made it this far without my leg cramping up entirely. I don't want to limp home.

Last time I visited him at this lookout, I ended up in his arms. We almost kissed. What might happen this time?

...Nothing, as it turns out. He's gone; his Jeep is missing, and there's no scent of either coffee or Damon's fresh scent behind the blind.

Even though I don't get to see him, I feel a little better anyway. I know it's mostly because I managed to push my parents out of my head for a while and fill my thoughts with Damon instead. I was hoping to see him here...but I can tell, at least, that he hasn't left town.

Just knowing that he's close makes me feel safe and protected.

The tire tracks from his Jeep tell me everything I need to

know. They're so fresh that the prints still have their sharp edges. I look around his hideaway as I catch my breath, my disappointment slowly warming into a sense of hope.

He's still here. He's still patrolling. He's still spending his nights alone.

It's impossible not to smile a little at those thoughts. I hate the idea of him being lonely...but I would love to be the one to fix it. It's selfish and it's unrealistic. But I can't get the idea out of my head.

I don't know his history, why Damon always seems to be walking under a dark cloud. I don't know what it is that seems to haunt him. I know he was in Afghanistan, and I've seen his Purple Heart. He has no family, no one to spend holidays with, or to come home to. It might just be loneliness?

But sometimes, when I look at those intense, haunted eyes, I wonder what could have happened to him to make him like this? He almost seems like he's mourning something...or doing penance. He may never be comfortable enough with me to talk about it, but I'd like to think I could at least offer him some comfort—if he would only confide in me.

Maybe I'm too inexperienced to understand whatever hell he's been through. But that's okay. I don't have to understand fully in order to care about and support him.

I just wish I could make him understand that.

As I stand there, my heart sinks a little again, and I miss him keenly. I thought this would be my chance to see him again. For two years, I've stayed away except for brief Christmas visits. I haven't seen him in all that time, and all I really want to do is feast my eyes on him one more time.

Well, that's not all I want. But it would be a nice start.

I know my therapist at the school clinic would have a field day if I ever told her about my crush on Damon. She would probably say something completely pointless about my interest in emotionally unavailable older men. But Damon is nothing like my father, which is part of why I fell for him.

He may be stoic, older, and isolated, but he's been so supportive—almost tender—with me. Even though as a kid I wished he would steal me away from my terrible parents and adopt me, I'm glad he never did. My heart sees him much differently now.

I sit down on the tree stump that he usually uses as a perch and sigh, resting my leg for a few minutes. Just being here makes my skin tingle. His secret place...that for a few short months was *our* secret place.

I miss him so much that for a moment my eyes sting and my heart aches. He's the only person in my life, aside from a few new friends in Denver, who has ever truly given a damn about me. I've tried to distract myself with boys my own age, but...next to his memory, they're not appealing at all.

In fact, they're tiresome: too eager to grab sensitive parts of my body with rough, greedy, little unwashed hands, too eager to show their dicks, too eager to demand sexual service that even porn actresses demand extra pay for, too angry when I say no.

I look at the stars twinkling from between the evergreen branches and sigh softly. *I'm never going to get over you, Damon. You've set the bar too high.*

Even though, with boys my age, you could set the bar on the ground and they'd dig to go under it.

My loneliness starts to settle back over me, like a weight being lowered by crane, when I hear the sound of a strong diesel engine coming up the hill. My heart leaps. *He's coming back!*

I knew he missed me! I hurry out from behind the bushes—and freeze, embarrassed, as a pair of headlights splash over me.

Shit, that's not him.

The white van in front of me looks almost new, aside from the scratches and dents on the sides and corners that imply its owner is a very bad driver. I'm backing up, praying the driver didn't see me scurry out of the bushes with a big, stupid smile on my face, when the van skids to a stop.

My smile fades as I back up further, suddenly too aware of the fact that I'm alone on a hill with a bad leg. I'm about to duck back into the woods when the passenger door and the side door open simultaneously and three guys in pale jeans and white hoodies step out.

"No need to stop for me," I call cheerily as I back up a bit more. "Just waiting for someone!" *Fuck.*

The one from the passenger seat looks at me with flat blue eyes, most of his face obscured by his hoodie, which is cinched tight. "Grab her. I wanna start fucking."

I freeze for a split second as they stride purposefully toward me. I can see the driver watching from his seat, the engine still running, poised to take off the moment they stuff me in the back.

The thing is, though, I don't just train in running. In only seconds, my shock wears off as cold anger floods my system with adrenaline. *Oh, so that's how it is.*

Damon taught me some basic self-defense during those months we got to know each other. He seemed determined to keep the whole thing as a platonic mentorship, and combat was a subject he was shockingly comfortable with. Because the lessons came from him, and I wanted so badly to impress him, I paid strict attention.

Once I was in Denver, I started taking classes. And practicing. I wanted to make sure that when I saw Damon again, I would be able to impress him.

Apparently, now it's time to use what I've learned. I duck back into Damon's hiding place, which is heavily cloaked in shadow. I know the terrain. I'm gambling that they don't.

"Fuck!" The guy yells. "Grab her, grab her!"

I can't run with my leg like this. That means hiding or fighting. Or maybe a bit of both.

As the two guys bull after me, one of them pushes directly through the bushes to cut me off and gets caught in the camouflage netting just behind it. He trips over it face-first, legs hopelessly tangled, and I scoop up a fallen pine branch and smash it over his head.

He jerks once and goes still as the pine bough snaps. I leave the pieces lying over him and get my guard up as I hear the second one cursing as he rushes after me.

In two years, you can't learn all that much. But dedicated practice of the basics can get you pretty far, especially when you're facing off against cocky boys who don't expect anyone with boobs to actually fight back. Determination washes away my fear as I look the skinny fool in his colorless eyes.

I step sharply aside as the idiot runs and reaches for me. His tackle failing, he flies past me, and I try to trip him on the way. He stumbles, managing to duck my back-fist, and then turns to attack me outright—not trying to grab me anymore, but simply lashing out with his fists.

My leg throbs with complaint, hobbling my footwork and forcing me to stand my ground. I duck, step backward, and with my left arm, redirect one of his blows right into a tree trunk beside my head. He yells in pain and stumbles back, holding his abused hand.

"Nice try," I mock him, brimming over with hate for these would-be rapists. He glares at me, cradling his hand. The guy on the ground lets out a low groan.

Damon would be proud of me right now, I think almost gleefully as I back further into the woods.

The third man comes rushing into the clearing, jumping through the gap his friend made, and then almost tripping over him.

"What the fuck is going on?" he demands. Once he sees the carnage, he abruptly stops, staring.

"You boys need to fuck off right now, or they're gonna be arresting you at the hospital." I call out, pitching my tone low and hard. Both guys still on their feet stop in midstep. After mimicking Damon since I was ten, my Scary Voice is pretty intimidating.

The wounded one reaches back to help untangle his semi-conscious friend from the blind as the guy from the passenger's seat continues to approach me, hands out. "Now come on, calm down. Be a good girl. This doesn't have to hurt if you're nice enough to us."

"Oh, it'll hurt. It'll hurt you." I bring up my fists, and when he makes a fast move for me, I fake a punch at his face—and then bring my unwounded leg up knee-first into his groin.

Retreating and ignoring the growing pain in my leg, I let him stumble away as he clutches his testicles. There's part of me that wants to loop the leather strap of my shoulder bag around his neck and start strangling. But that's murder, and I just want to defend myself.

Suddenly, he yells in anger and makes a swift grab for my legs—and the knee on my bad leg gives out as his grip yanks it to the side. I gasp in pain and horror as I go down.

I lash out with my good leg, kicking him hard in the jaw as I scream at the top of my lungs. I keep landing blow after blow on his head and shoulders, but he hangs on, cursing, even after I have him spitting blood. *What the fuck is this guy's skull made of, solid rock?*

His mouth is dripping gore, and one eye is swelling shut, but he still won't stop. He's yanking me by my bad leg, sending agony through my entire body as he drags me so I am beneath him. Once my face is within reach, he starts raining blows down on me.

"Cunt!" he pants. "Slut! I'm gonna make you choke on this dick for that!"

For one horrifying moment, I think, *I'm going to lose. I'm going to get raped by this pile of pig shit and his friends. They'll probably record it and upload it on social media, and then a million sociopathic fuckboys and incels will laugh at me online.*

Just as I spot the other two assailants start to crouch forward in eager anticipation, their bodies get etched out in silhouette by a pair of bright white headlights, and I hear the scream of tires.

Steel and glass smash together, and I see the van get slammed into sight on the far edge of the bushes as all three boys look up in shock.

I yank back the fucker's hoodie and get a good look at his face: pale skin, ruddy cheeks, a long, plain face, flat blue eyes, blond curls. I memorize it. Then I slam both palms hard over his ears.

He grunts in pain, grabbing his head and falling to the side as I pull free. *Too bad it didn't kill him*, I catch myself thinking fiercely, and I yank myself to my feet with the help of a tree trunk.

But that's as far as I make it. My leg throbs so sharply I'm scared he's broken it again. I know at once it won't support even part of my weight. I'm stuck.

The one with the injured hand heads for me as the third one starts to scrabble away from the cold bright glare. I brace myself, knowing I can't dodge.

Then a tall figure lunges suddenly through the gap in the bushes, leaping over the two on the ground and yanks the asshole away from me before I can blink. He slams the kid face first against a tree once, twice, and then lets him go. The boy staggers back, shaking his head, the front of his hoodie spattered with blood.

"You! Who are you? What the hell do you think you're doing

here?" Damon demands, his voice harsh and terrifying with rage.

"Run for it, you stupid fucks! He'll kill you!" From the van, the driver screams his warning, his voice cracking in fear like a young teen's.

The boys bolt, two staggering, one limping away holding his groin. With whiplash speed, Damon grabs the blond by the shoulder before he's out of reach and slams him against a tree, staring into his face. "Who are you?" he demands again. "Who the fuck raised you?"

The boy whines wordlessly in fear as he squirms—and then something that surprises even Damon with its inventive cowardice. He slides sideways and down, letting his arms go limp, and slips right out of his hoodie like a greased rat.

Damon drops the empty piece of clothing and twists after him, but if there's one thing these boys seem good at, it's running from consequences. They scatter around the brush and scramble away. Damon gives chase, vanishing from my sight. I can't see what's happening! Moments later, I hear the van doors slam and the van screeching away.

Over the pounding of my heart, I make out the sounds of Damon's Jeep engine refusing to turn over and his angry sigh.

Suddenly my cheeks are burning. *I screwed up and he had to rescue me. Sorry, Damon.* I went running in the middle of the night and ended up in trouble. It should have been fine, but I've been living in Denver the last two years. Maybe things have changed around the Butte. Maybe I should have known better.

I test my weight on my leg and have to quickly grab the tree again. The pain is a little less intense, but I still can't walk. My leg feels locked up.

I brace myself for an accusation when Damon comes hurrying back to me. He's even bigger and more intense than I remember, like a wolf stalking toward me out of the woods. The light gleams off his hair and his light leather jacket and shines across his eyes as they fix on me.

"Are you all right?" he asks urgently.

A lump forms in my throat. I was preparing myself for rejection and condemnation—just as I always do. My parents taught me that. Instead, Damon moves forward and crouches beside me, gently laying his hands on my wounded leg.

The pain has settled down to a dull throb. The warmth of his hands through my pants soothes me, and I let out a contented sigh before I can stop myself. "I am now," I manage. "Thank you."

"You shouldn't have waited up here for me," he reproaches in such a gentle voice that I blush. "If I hadn't doubled back…"

"But you did," I murmur as he straightens, towering over me. He's standing so close to me that I can feel the heat coming off his skin through his shirt. His scent is an intoxicating mix of clean laundry and leather. "You're always there when I need you."

His fierce eyes narrow sensually. For a moment, I think I hear a shudder in his breath and wonder in sweet agony if he's finally going to kiss me.

But of course, he doesn't. "Can you walk?"

"My leg's too wobbly. I'm worried it's reinjured." I am less worried now, but I still don't understand why it won't take my weight.

"You're having a muscle spasm. I'll check you more thoroughly once we get somewhere safe." Without warning, Damon scoops me up into his arms, He does it so easily that I gasp aloud in surprise, and he starts carrying me back toward his Jeep. "I'll call my assistant to bring a car."

The trek to the road in his embrace takes only two desperate, trembling heartbeats. I cling to his neck the whole time, breathless, gazing up at him as he looks purposefully at the dented

Jeep. Too soon, he's settling me carefully on the seat with my legs stretched out.

When he lets go of me, I want to cry out. But I just smile up at him bravely and nod when he tells me to hang in there.

His assistant turns out to be a calm, professionally-mannered man in his thirties with reddish-blond hair. He looks like he could be an ex-biker. Patrick brings a dark sedan and stays with the Jeep while Damon drives us away.

To my surprise, he doesn't turn toward my house. He turns toward the Tower. My heart flutters as we make our way up the mountainside toward that single spire.

I am finally going to see the inside of his home. But what's going to happen once I'm there?

CHAPTER 4

Damon

Amy smells so sweet and sensual, the faint, musky scent of sweat from her run mixing with the soft fruit and floral hints of her shampoo. My cock aches with need the whole time that I carry her back to the Jeep, and my arms ache with loss when I settle her on its seat. My hands clench in frustration as I walk around to the driver's side door.

She's looking at me that way again—like I'm her only hero and the only man she wants. I don't know if it's her adoration or my thirst that worries me more. It's just like it was back when she was eighteen...but she's grown even more beautiful.

"I'm sorry. I should have called and warned you when I found out that a group of boys were out hassling women around town." It's the truth, but I only realize it in hindsight. "I didn't think you would run so far with your leg still healing." I can't quite keep the edge out of my voice.

She sighs and nods slowly. "I'm sorry. I didn't even expect to be out tonight. But my mom, she just..." Amy's voice trails off.

"Made it impossible for you to stay?" I ask quietly.

She swallows hard and nods, not saying anything. She doesn't have to.

I hate her mother. Annabeth has always been a hysterical, selfish, manipulative bitch. She was when we went to school together, she was when she married George Gatlin, but when she had poor Amy, she really went off the rails.

The thing is, she's always just been a drama queen—until she hooked up with George. Now, she's the sidekick to someone much, much worse.

George is really the dangerous one. He reminds me in some ways of those boys: a coward, hungry to do horrible things, but terrified of being caught. If it wasn't for the fact that I couldn't trust myself to get too involved in others' lives, I would have taken Amy away from him a long time ago.

As it is, I've had him watched for years. I know that Annabeth got pregnant with Amy to trap George into marriage, and George, being even less rational than his wife, blames Amy. I know that Annabeth is scared of George, and that where she's all talk, he's actually a doer.

I know that the only reason Amy is in college now, instead of having simply been thrown out of their house at age eighteen, is because I instructed them to play at being responsible parents while I footed the damn bill.

George isn't just a dud as a father. He's an angry, nasty little boy with no maturity, no balls, and no limits on what he'll do if he thinks he can get away with it. And with the foster system as the only other alternative, I've had to force him and his idiotic wife to look after Amy properly.

And they've still managed to break her heart.

"Do you know who those boys were?" Her shaky voice tears me away from my reminiscing. I shake my head.

"No. I've only seen one's face so far. I'll have to track them down. Good thing it's a small town." When I find that blond fucking brat I'm going to have to fight the urge to punch his teeth down his throat for putting his hands on Amy. But better to toss his ass in jail.

"Could they be tourists?" She sounds almost hopeful, and I can understand why. Better strangers from out of town than her neighbors' kids—people she grew up with.

"Maybe, but I don't think so. They knew the streets well enough to avoid me. These people live here—whoever they are."

I look her way and see her shivering, her arms wrapped around herself despite the warm night. "Look, I'll find them. Just trust me on that one."

"I do," she says, and despite her fear, her tone is so tender that it makes me ache all over again. "I just don't understand why they did that. Why they're like this." Her voice cracks a little, and I feel my throat tighten.

"Try not to worry yourself with trying to make sense of it. They're probably just a bunch of brats who've never had to face consequences for anything, who figure Daddy's money can get them out of any trouble, and who don't really see women or girls as human. That's it." I speak with gentle authority, my tone firm as we turn onto my private drive.

"Good. So it wasn't anything I did?" There's a tiny hint of self-reproach in her voice. It makes me wince. I have to squash any thought that she's to blame—especially since I'm the one who could have warned her and prevented it all from happening.

"No. Wrong place, wrong time. They were clearly driving around looking for someone they could grab off the street. But this isn't Denver. There aren't too many people out after dark, let alone women or girls walking around alone."

As I slow down to enter the circular drive at the base of the tower, I glance over at her to see that she's relaxing a little and nodding. "I want you to stop going on these night runs until those boys are safely in jail. They're arrogant as well as pathological. They may try to target you again out of revenge."

"Of course, I understand," she murmurs, sounding disappointed. I know why. It's not just the exercise that she'll miss.

She confirms it just a moment later. "How will I get to see you, then?"

I sigh. It's our first time together in two years, and all I should be thinking about is getting her leg attended to and packing her off home. But that's not what I want. It's what I dutifully try to tell myself I should do.

"You shouldn't be seeing me, Amy. I keep trying to tell you. You deserve a better guy than I can be—someone young and kind."

"You always say that," she complains gently, and I sigh again as I pull to a stop outside the tall, oak double door.

"That's because it's true. I'm a burned-out military guy twice your age. You're too damn good for me. Too kind, too innocent." Her lovely eyes seem to plead silently with me. I tear my gaze away with all the strength of will I can muster. "I'll fucking get you dirty, Amy."

She smiles, maddeningly and invitingly all at once. "Maybe that's what I want."

I don't have a comeback for that, so I focus on parking and then carrying her inside. I have to keep steering my thoughts away from sex and the warmth of her body as I bundle her against me. Her soft breath on my neck as she lays her head on my shoulder makes it all that much harder.

"Looks like you fought back hard," I manage as I carry her in over the threshold. "Good for you. I'm certain it made the difference." No point in bringing up what difference that was. She doesn't need reminding that she was nearly gang-raped.

She doesn't answer but is suddenly quiet as her head swivels to look around at the stonework. The Tower was a personal project of mine, built six stories tall and faced and floored with red Colorado sandstone. The entryway shows off the great hall that takes up the bottom floor and the sweep of the grand staircase that spirals upward through all six floors—from sub-basement to rooftop.

"I used to wonder what it was like in here," she finally breathes as she gazes around. "It's a lot bigger than I expected."

"I'll give you the tour as soon as your leg's feeling better." I'm glad she likes my home; I'm pretty proud of it. It's got an interesting mix of Hollywood Medieval and Southwestern Gothic with the arched windows and heavy tiled roof of a Mission-era church.

"I'd like that." She takes a deep breath. "I started self-defense training in college. Denver gets dangerous at night sometimes, and I wanted to build on what you taught me." She presses closer to me as I make my way up the stairs, and I almost stumble.

"Good," I manage, my heart pounding in my chest so hard that I'm sure she can feel it. I silently pray that she can't feel the pounding in my groin. It's clear now that she's never gotten over me either.

I can't let her get hurt. Especially not by me. I carry her up one floor to my office and settle her onto the tobacco-colored leather couch. "How are you feeling?"

She gazes into my eyes, and I see everything there that I want to see but can't afford to notice. My heart leaps, a bolt of adrenaline shoots through me, and for a moment it's all I can do not to lean over and kiss her.

Her leg. Her leg is injured and I have to check it. I straighten, taking a deep breath.

"Okay, I need to have a closer look at your leg. If we're lucky, you won't need to go to the hospital, just some strong muscle rub and some rest. If we're not, I'll get you back to the car right away."

She bites her lip and nods up at me, eyes a little wider. "Okay, what do I do?"

"I need to get your pants off."

Her eyes light up and a huge grin spreads over her face. I barely stop myself from covering my face with my hand. *I walked right into that.* "Very funny. Either they come off, or I'll have to cut one of the pant legs open."

"Oh." Her smile fades slightly. "Okay."

She lifts her hips, and I gently tug off her pants, trying to ignore the sight of her gleaming thighs as they emerge from the gray sweatpants. But even as I pull off her trainers and socks and finish stripping her injured leg, my head is starting to pound along with everything else.

Sweet Lord give me strength. Her bare legs may have lost some muscle thanks to her injury, but they are polished and strong, the skin so smooth that I have to snatch my hand away. And there's suddenly so much skin to look at.

She's wearing a tiny, sleek running thong in the same blue as her tank top, and it only takes a glimpse of the high-tech fabric clinging to the mound of her pussy to leave me shaking a little. *Fuck. Control yourself, idiot!*

"Does it hurt?" I murmur as I force myself to start examining her leg. The muscles are tight still, but no longer locked in a spasm. One or two feel pulled, and she has some bruises forming.

"No," she breathes.

No breaks, no sprains, and I don't feel anything out of alignment. "You have some pulled muscles, and your whole leg was tensed in a spasm before. Probably why you couldn't walk on it. If you rest it for a day or so, you'll be fine."

I catch myself running my hand gently over her soft skin, as if I can somehow caress her pain away. I quickly stop myself and ignore the sudden constriction in my chest.

She draws in a shivering breath, and I look up with her calf still in my hand. She's lying there on the couch, looking ready to swoon. Her eyes are closed, her lips parted, her lovely breasts are heaving, and she seems so entranced by the touch of my hands that I know in that moment that she's completely in my power.

Or rather, we're both rapidly falling under the power of something much stronger than either of us. The realization alarms me. I can smell the delicate musk of arousal rising from between her slim thighs, and my breath comes out in a soft agonized groan.

I can't. I move back, letting her go, and she sits up, her eyes hazy with confusion.

"You have to understand," I say, talking fast even as I feel tingling heat spread outward from my groin. I'm breathing heavily, my voice low and almost pleading. "I keep telling you that you wouldn't want me even half so much if you really knew me."

"Then tell me about yourself," she insists softly as I struggle to massage her bare leg with shaking hands. "Let me make my own damn decision about you. Tell me everything."

I swallow hard. It's the only option I have left, besides climbing onto that Goddamn couch and letting her keep her illusions. Like a coward and a liar would.

I'm neither of those—never have been, never will be. That means I can forget about ever having her for good. After all, once she realizes that I'm worse than her father could ever dream of being, and that my gifts to her are all born of a guilty need to protect the innocent, her crush on me will die.

And that's going to be a knife in the gut, no matter how good my intentions.

But she's absolutely right; this absolutely needs to happen.

Full fucking disclosure. Then she can walk away understanding that I'm just trying to avoid hurting her.

Not that I would ever lift a finger against her. But I know that when she learns the difference between the man she thinks she loves and the man standing just behind that illusion, she'll be disappointed. "I'm sorry," I say quietly.

"For what?" Her eyes are so soft and innocent as she watches me, her healthy leg drawn up artlessly with her arm propped on top of it. "For rescuing me when no one else would? Or for not touching me when we both want you to?"

Now her eyes challenge me. I look away first, surprising myself. Women don't usually get the better of me...but I can't lie to her, and I can't hide my feelings, either. *Fuck.*

All the more reason to keep my distance. It seems like we're dangerous for each other. *Why hasn't she gotten dressed? I should tell her to put her pants back on.*

I don't say any such thing.

"I was a soldier like I told you," I say slowly as I settle into a nearby chair. My whole body aches now, like I'm starving myself of something essential—air, food, rest? *Her.* "But you don't become wealthy as a soldier, and I had no family to fall back on."

I cough out a laugh. "Well, none to speak of. None that would have had my back on anything. My father was a lot more active in his malice than yours, believe me."

"I'm sorry," she says, and her soft voice is like a balm to me. I have to ignore that—and the fresh wave of desire that it brings.

I know that I could rest for a while in her arms and even find peace. But who am I to ask for peace?

I hand her a small pot of muscle rub, and she starts smoothing it into her leg in a way that makes my breath catch in my chest. "I guess I thought you just had a rich family or something."

"No, they were dirt poor. I didn't even put myself through college until I was well out on my own, and the old man was dead." I smile at her, a little lopsided. The sensual haze has lifted from her eyes a little.

"I became a mercenary after Afghanistan. I had nothing to go home to. I sure didn't have anyone to stick around for. I had cut all ties. So I started fighting for money. And believe me, business was good."

I'm watching her face. She looks back at me curiously, the light is still in her eyes—the light that always, inexplicably, shines for me. "So you worked for a military contractor?"

"At first. Then I worked freelance. I developed a reputation for doing discreet work in high-security locations."

It still hasn't dawned on her. "First as part of a small team and then alone. First it was rescues, extractions. Then they started using me for wet work."

I'm still watching her face. I'm watching it dawn on her; I can see the realization take over her expression. The shock at first. Then the horror—surprisingly mild—but still there.

I brace myself for the disgust. "I got very good at it, Amy."

"You're an assassin for hire." Her voice sounds breathless, and more than a little incredulous. I don't blame her for that. It's a crazy story, especially to someone whose life and ordeals have been a lot less bloody.

"I was. I quit. I made enough money, and I couldn't stomach it any more.

"That's when I came home...and found out that the Butte was having problems." I look down at my hands and then slowly back up at her. Still no disgust. *Why?*

"So you decided to help us." She swallows and leans toward me. I try to ignore the glimpse of cleavage that's revealed, just like I try to ignore everything else, but I'm so dizzy with lust I can barely keep it together. "And I'm supposed to hate you, for going from a killer to the guy who has saved me multiple times?"

I blink at her in absolute amazement. "Amy...you should judge a man by the sum of his deeds, not just what he's done lately. The people I killed are still dead."

"And the people you have saved are still alive and well," she says, and she rises from the couch, moving toward me unsteadily. I freeze in my chair, my warning to spare her leg dying in my throat as she closes the distance and cups my face in her soft little hands.

"And that means me too. Damon...I'm not dismissing what you're saying to me—that you used to kill people for money. Okay? I hear you loud and clear."

I grunt in response, my heart banging away in my ears, my body frozen as she touches me. *Amy...Amy, don't...*

"But you're the only one who has ever really given a damn about me in this town. You saved my life; you made me feel safe. And you went and did it again tonight."

There are tears in her eyes. I can't stand to see them. My hand moves by itself and brushes them lightly off her cheeks as they fall.

Then she leans forward to hug me, her arms slipping down from my cheeks to wrap around my shoulders. And suddenly I realize that she's not going to look at me with horror or disgust.

Maybe she's naive. Maybe she's too deeply infatuated with who she thinks I am. Maybe she's far too forgiving and kind than a man like me deserves. But suddenly, my need for her overrules my reason, and I stand up and pull her into my arms.

CHAPTER 5

Amy

Before today, I didn't know that Damon was carrying a torch for me, just as I have been for him. In all my wishful fantasies, I never imagined he might return even half my feelings. I had no idea how much emotion he was fighting until he's crushing me against him like a drowning man grabbing a lifesaver. It's just a little too tight...but that added pressure turns me on even more as I hug him back as hard as I can.

HE'S MUTTERING something into my hair, and I can feel his heart pounding against my breasts. The storm in my head is too loud for a moment for me to figure out what he's saying. Then I manage to catch my breath and finally realize that he's repeating in a low, desperate voice, "I can't do this."

My heart drops. *Yes you can*, I want to say. But after what just happened, I'm sensitive about pushing his limits. One glorious night isn't worth him hating us both for it afterward.

I LIFT my head and look up at him. I drag my gaze from his sensual mouth up to his eyes. It takes every bit of self-control I have not to kiss him, and from the tremors going through his big, warm body, I know he feels the same. "Damon...I can't say I love you and then push you into something you don't want."

HIS EYES FILL with desperate conflict. But then, seemingly with all his strength, he lets me go, making sure I can stand before he releases me fully.

"I NEED TO GET YOU HOME," he says breathlessly, and I swallow back my tears and nod.

I DON'T REALIZE how badly the near miss with those boys had shaken me until I am dropped back at my house. My parents have already gone to sleep. I take a shower in the downstairs bathroom and realize I've been standing there scrubbing myself for almost ten minutes when the hot water starts to go tepid.

DAMN IT. I hate the idea that those boys affected me so much. But without Damon around to distract me with his fierce but gentle masculinity, I'm stuck remembering those violent little creeps trying to grab me so they could rape me, and then beating on me when they didn't get their way.

. . .

I HAVE a bruise developing on my cheek and defensive bruises on my forearms. My leg is stiff and my knee hurts, but the muscle rub Damon gave me helped. Thankfully he sent me home with the jar. I use the rub on my leg some more, ice my bruises and put comfrey oil on them before crawling into bed.

I LIE THERE UNTIL DAWN, dozing a bit but otherwise restless. I don't know what bothers me more: the memory of those bastards touching me or the absence of Damon's hands on me right now.

IF I CAN JUST FIND a way to show him that I believe in him, that I'm not scared, and that the man he is now deserves love just like almost everyone else, then maybe we can have each other. It's not like he kills people now.

IF HE DID, that would be a deal-breaker, but I know that's not the case. He saves lives now; he doesn't take them.

THE FIRST THING I do in the morning is check my bank accounts on my laptop. My parents give me no allowance above board and tuition, but I have an on-campus job and have managed to save a few hundred over last semester. It's mostly still there.

I'M FEELING tempted to pull the money out and book a couple of weeks at one of the bed and breakfasts just to get a break from the couple currently having breakfast downstairs. I know I'm in for an awkward talk as it is, once Mom sees the bruises. But I resist the temptation for now. If I can hold out for a few more weeks, I can end my stay in town on my own terms—and being able to look forward to that will make it easier to hold out for it.

WHEN I GO DOWNSTAIRS, I see my father hunker deeper behind his tablet, shoulders almost up to his ears, as if he resents no longer having a proper newspaper to hide behind. My mother is picking at her eggs; her jaw drops when she sees me. "What the hell happened to you?"

I STARE BACK AT HER, expressionless. "Have you watched the local news this morning?" I ask in a cold tone.

SHE BLINKS at me and then turns on the television. Our local news station covers nothing but weather, local events, and emergencies, and only broadcasts during daytime hours. Right now, Charlie, our local reporter, actually sounds excited.

"AN INNOCENT SLEEPOVER *turned into a near nightmare when one of the three girls was nearly kidnapped during a snack run at the Mountain Avenue gas station...*"

MY FATHER LOWERS his tablet and lifts an eyebrow. I ignore him; he makes it easy. "They didn't just go after that one girl," I say quietly.

MY MOTHER GIVES me a confused look before turning back to the screen, where the broadcast went from covering the gas station to showing an unfamiliar street back in the woods.

"Forty-five minutes later, *Alexandra Mason, age twenty-four, was out walking her Newfoundland dog Blackberry on Pine Lane when the same white van pulled up alongside her. Two of the men, whom she described as "dirtied and bruised," were wearing bandannas tied around their faces and opened the side door to try and pull her in. It was then that Blackberry sprang into action.*"

I let out a laugh. Apparently after Damon and I had pummeled them, they still tried again with someone else. And now they could add dog bites to their list of injuries. "Those assholes tried to grab me too."

I show my mother the finger-shaped bruises on my upper arm from where one of them had grabbed me, and she covered her mouth with her hands, eyes wide. For a moment, I glimpse some humanity there. But then she asks skeptically, "You took on four of them yourself and drove them away?"

My father seems to freeze, his puzzlement turning to astonishment and then a sort of fear. I look past Mom's shoulder directly at him and say simply, "Of course. I've been training hard. And I'm tired of cowardly bullies who hate women."

My mother sits the fuck back down and just stares at the television as the horrible but somewhat comedic story of those idiots' complete inability to secure a victim unfolds. They haven't been identified yet, but somehow, after the fifteen-year-old, every single woman they tried to attack took a piece of them. Or her dog did.

Or the haunted, badass love of her life did.

Smirking, my leg suddenly barely hurting at all, I walk right past my parents and into the kitchen to make myself a sandwich for the road. I still ache for Damon...but I have some hope now that he'll come around. I just have to hold out until he does.

CHPATER 6

Damon

It takes me less than half an hour to find the dull-eyed blond who put his hands on my Amy. He stares out at me from his yearbook photo, a cocky smile set on his face, but his eyes so empty that they make his expression look fake. Chad Evanston, currently age nineteen. Possibly a sociopath, definitely a vile little shit.

He was in the class behind Amy, with rich parents, an influential family, and a juvenile record as long as my arm. He was never actually punished for any of it. His father saw to that.

I wonder what his father will say when I talk this over with him. I have a suspicion: *Not my son. No, absolutely not my boy.* Like every other parent of a destructive little shit, he'll likely deny it. But sometimes, someone close to a loose cannon cares enough to do something.

I have to try.

The background research doesn't take long. Guys in his age bracket tend to either be very vigilantly private or all out in the open with barely any information security at all. Chad is the latter, and that makes my job much easier.

I'm distracted though, which means it takes me longer than normal. My mind keeps drifting back to Amy and the moment last night when I almost carried her off to my bed. I know that whether I end up fucking her or not, I'm going to regret it either way. The problem is I don't want her to regret sleeping with me.

But the way she reacted last night…it was like I was breaking her heart by refusing her. And yet, she backed off as soon as she sensed something was really wrong. She was right to do so; I still can't get past the feeling that she'll flee as soon as what I told her really sinks in.

That girl could have me wrapped around her finger without any effort at all, and I know I could sway her almost as easily. We're each other's weakness. But there's something in me that wishes we could be each other's strength instead.

No matter what I do about Amy, it won't happen until after I catch this little bastard and his friends. They belong in jail, and their parents need a talking-to about what kind of young men they are raising in my town.

Chad Evanston is the kind of low-promise boy who coasts by on his father's money and nepotism. His Facebook profile is full of a strange mix of rap videos, suggestive images of girls and women, anti-feminist memes, and reposts celebrating gang life. He seems to fancy himself an up-and-coming criminal mastermind.

After another half an hour, I know everything about him: his C average at State, his string of moving violations and drunk and disorderly charges, his equally embarrassing string of break-ups, usually occurring roughly two weeks apart from each other.

His address.

This boy is ruining every damned chance he has to get a leg

up in life as if he's refusing to grow up altogether. And now he's trying to reinvent himself as the baddest man in the Butte.

Too bad that title's already taken, you sad little fuck.

I want to kill him, but again find myself thinking back to Amy and her faith in me. If there's any chance that the man I am now is acceptable to her, I refuse to blow it all by bloodying my hands again. I want to be that better man she thinks I am, even if I never get to touch her.

I consider calling the deputy, but he's probably dealing with all the extra traffic from the tourists coming through. Besides...I want to handle this myself.

Everyone in town knows what it means when I pay an unexpected visit to one of their houses. Either someone needs my help or someone there is fucking up. So when Evanston's father, a tallish, chubby man in a brown plaid golfing outfit, answers the door of their sprawling outskirts house, he pales a little at the sight of me.

"Mr. Evanston, I need to talk to you about your son and his new hobby of choice," I say very calmly.

His lips tremble, and he mops his suddenly sweaty face. "Chad's not here. I haven't seen him since last night after dinner. He's at that age, you know—he comes and goes."

I nod slowly, staring solemnly into his eyes. I can see the fear and resentment there—and the craftiness, too. He's hiding something.

"Mr. Evanston, there is security footage and eyewitness accounts of your son attempting multiple kidnappings with some of his friends last night. If you know something—"

"Whatever people are saying, it's all lies. That was someone else's kid." His face goes red, and his eyes are suddenly just as blank as his son's.

"I'll be leaving that up to the courts. You should just know that your son intended to—" I stop dead as my phone starts to ring. It's a ringtone I set a long time ago, back when Amy first got her cellphone and insisted that I take the number.

She's calling me now.

A jab of alarm goes through me, and I look back at Evanston briefly. "If you see the boy, for God's sake, don't let him go out with his friends tonight. He's going to end up in prison otherwise."

The man says nothing at all in reply, just stares at me as I turn and stalk back down the walk. I return Amy's call as soon as I'm shut up inside my sedan. "Amy? Is everything all right?"

The first sound I hear is a sob, and my heart clenches. "I need you to come get me," she gasps out.

I stiffen, hearing noises in the background that worry me more and more: thuds, the crackle of a fire, her mother screaming in rage. "Amy, what the hell is going on?"

I hear her take a deep breath as she struggles for composure. "Those boys torched my car and my dad's car, and now my parents are throwing me out for bringing trouble to their doorstep."

Hot anger floods my system. "I'll be right over."

When I get there, it's worse than I imagined. Both her compact and her father's sedan are smoking shells being hosed down by the fire department. Someone has burned the word *SLUT* into her parents' lawn with lighter fluid, and both front windows are broken. Her father is standing at her second floor bedroom window unceremoniously dumping her every personal belonging onto what is left of the lawn.

Amy stands on the sidewalk, hands over her face, while her mother hovers over her squawking like a large, angry chicken. Just the sight of her bullying her daughter makes me want to strangle her to death. I come screeching up at the curb beside them, and both her parents freeze.

I get out of the car, pull Amy's mother away from Amy and point a finger in her face. "Shut the fuck up."

She does, her mouth closing with an audible snap. I nod, my fury easing a fraction. "Now go inside. Don't let me see your face or that of your coward husband again."

It's not a request. She takes one look at my eyes and turns around, waddling inside on feet swollen from an entire day spent in bad fuck-me heels. I turn my gaze to the second-floor window, but the coward in question has already vanished inside.

One of the firefighters is gathering up the least broken of Amy's belongings, while the rest of the team packs up and sympathetically grumble over what dicks Amy's parents are. I turn to her, walking up and laying my hands on her shoulders.

She turns to me at once and throws herself into my arms.

Only then does she really fall apart; I know she's been holding it in to keep her mother from tearing into her even harder. I ignore the pleasurable jolt that goes through my body and hold her tight, letting her cling to me until she gets her crying under control.

As I wait, I look up at the upstairs window again and see Amy's father standing there, staring at me apprehensively. I stare back at him and mouth two words.

Leave town.

His eyes widen, and then his colorless face disappears from the window as I turn to lead Amy back to my car.

"You're staying with me until you're well," I tell her firmly as I bring her and her belongings up the mountain road to my tower home. She nods mutely, her cheeks still wet. I hate seeing her like this, so much that I know someone is going to suffer for it.

I'm concerned by how angry I am on Amy's behalf. I worry that these vermin are going to drive me to violence. I have to protect her, no matter what.

But I can't kill again. I swore to her last night that that life was behind me.

When we get back to the Tower, I bring her up to my office again and sit there holding her hand while I call the deputy.

He's already gotten a call from the County about the arson investigation. I give him the information about the Evanstons and make him promise to tell me about any new developments. I'm so angry that after I hang up, I have to sit with my eyes closed for a while to calm down before I can turn a look of sympathy toward Amy.

She shakes her head when I ask if she's all right. "I can't be," she whispers. "After this, there's no health insurance, no college, no nothing. They're disowning me—dropping me on my ass. Dad's calling a lawyer tomorrow."

Blind anger washes through me as I think of that cowardly little bully and all the tears he's caused her over the years. *And all for what? I will never truly understand men like this.*

I do know that he won't go so far as to make the calls to get a restraining order against her. It would make him look bad. He'll just change the locks, change their phone numbers, and maybe even plot something nasty in case Amy insists on showing up.

But what makes me rage is that he and his yapping lap-dog of a wife would make Amy believe such things and lock her out entirely, when she is wounded and hunted and scared. *Monsters.*

Some of that anger turns back on me immediately. *I should have taken her from him a decade ago, even if I could never have raised her myself.*

"No, no, no, you're going to be fine," I say hurriedly, knowing that if I no longer have to force her parents to pretend to be decent, I can at least give her the whole truth. "Your physical therapy's paid for, and your tuition is covered until you graduate."

She blinks up at me, too startled to continue weeping. "What are you talking about?"

"I've been paying for both," I explain. "I've been doing my best over the years to make sure you were provided for properly. I couldn't give you a decent childhood, and I knew what the foster system was like, so I tried to make the two of them do it.

"But it seems I made a mistake in thinking that I could force them to be decent parents. They always found ways to hurt you anyway. And now that you're an adult, and they're taking themselves out of the picture, I can at least be honest with you about it all."

I brace myself for her anger or confusion, knowing I deserve to be yelled at. I deceived her, even if it was well-meaning.

She gazes up at me for a long moment. "You keep talking about how terrible you are," she says softly. "You keep telling me how you don't deserve me. Not my love, not my loyalty, none of it. But you've earned it more than anyone I have ever met."

My throat tightens and I swallow hard. "Amy..."

She smiles up at me so sweetly, with such tenderness in her honey-colored eyes that my breath catches. I have no defense against her need for me.

When our lips brush, I can't tell who kissed who first. But I reach for her, crushing her berry-sweet lips against me to deepen the kiss and hear her soft whimper of pleasure. The sound caresses my ears, and I start to ache all over again...and I know that this time, I can't possibly resist.

And I don't want to.

CHAPTER 7

Amy

His kiss makes me weak; I feel myself being pulled fiercely across his lap, and I throw my arms around his neck, returning the kiss with desperate hunger. Our lips cling and slide together. I taste the mint and bourbon on his tongue, feel the faint rasp of his late-afternoon stubble, and start to tremble as his tongue teases against my lips.

I HEAR him panting hard through his nose, his breath shaky on my cheek, his hands trembling as they start to explore my back through my shirt. I want so badly to tear off that inconvenient fabric, but instead I just keep kissing him, savoring this moment.

HIS FINGERS clench in the back of my shirt as if he wants to tear it off of me as well. I feel a shudder go through him, and I know he's still fighting against his conscience a little. I hold him, stroking his back as the kiss breaks.

I FEEL like I'm teetering on the edge of a knife as he stays silent, head on my shoulder. Everything depends on him; I'll respect his limits, but I know my need won't go away—especially now that it's been made clear that he's the only one I've ever been able to rely on.

THEN SUDDENLY, he scoops me into his arms and stands, lifting me as if I weigh nothing at all. I curl up in his embrace, hanging on to him, and feel myself go dizzy and loose-limbed, as if I'm going to faint. *Oh God, yes.* A thrum of warmth pulses from my head to my toes.

MY HEAD IS WHIRLING as he carries me out to the landing and up the stairs. His muscles are taut, his grip just a little too tight, and I hear him breathing through his teeth as I cling to his massive shoulders. Up and up the spiral staircase, feeling like I'm going to start soaring, but at the same time aching more and more for him to pin me down.

I catch a brief glimpse of his bedroom as we burst into it. It's at the very top of the tower, surrounded by multi-paned windows that run floor to ceiling. The bed itself is round, curtained, and sits in the middle of this uppermost room under a skylight full of stars.

HE LAYS me down on the mattress and I stare up at the sky, entranced with the view. Damon's nearness soon fills my vision as he reaches for me, and I am so overwhelmed with bliss that for a while all I can do is lie there as he gently runs his hands over my arms and shoulders. My lungs burn sweetly as I struggle for air. When he starts kissing my neck, I gasp, lolling my head to the side in sweet submission.

"Do whatever you want to me," I croon. "But don't you dare stop..."

I bury my fingers in his hair, tugging him against me insistently as his teeth graze against my pulse. His breath is hot on my neck; he fastens his lips onto me and sucks delicately.

I moan, my hips writhing with each pull of his lips; he wraps his arms around me and then slides his hands up my back, taking my shirt with them. I raise my arms, squirming with delight as he slides the cloth off over my head, and then starts caressing my back while his mouth moves down my cleavage.

I have never had a man touch me like this before. My whole body relaxes; I feel his tongue slide over the upper curves of my breasts and then down between them, and my nipples start tingling with need. I gasp for air and arch my back, impatiently reaching back to undo my demure white cotton bra and push the straps off my shoulders.

"Mmm, someone wants me to stop teasing," he murmurs in a low, throaty voice. His tone is shaky with need, but the amusement behind it makes my cheeks burn and my lips curve into a smile. When I look up at him, the heat in his eyes is almost too intense for me to hold his gaze.

"Kiss them?" I ask very shyly as I pull the cloth from my breasts and toss the bra away.

He responds with a contented rumble. He kicks off his shoes and pulls off my trainers, and for a moment I wonder if he's going to tease me further by ignoring my request. I can't repeat it; it took all my nerve to ask the first time.

Then I notice that he's turned his eyes to me as he's peeling off his jeans. I watch mesmerized as he sides them down. The black boxer briefs beneath cling to his hips and sculpted ass and are stretched to their limit in front. I sit up, fascinated, wanting to touch the throbbing cock that's barely contained by that silky fabric.

My fingers reach to trail down his rippling belly…and then I find myself falling back again as he clambers onto the bed over me, straddling my legs and caging me in with his arms. He gazes at me with that fierce heat again…and then starts kissing his way up between my breasts, burying his face between them.

He lets out another low, contented groan as I wrap my arms around him, pressing my breasts together against his cheeks, and he turns his head hungrily to kiss one as I arch my back and offer them. The touch of his lips on my inexperienced skin makes me moan again, and I move my hands over him, going from gripping his hair to caressing his shoulders with grasping hands.

His mouth circles my nipple, trying out different caresses to test my response: a nibble, a trailing tongue, warm breath, soft kisses. Some of them make me gasp and tense; others make me sigh and relax under him. Finally, he spirals inward, sucking my aching nipple into his mouth firmly.

"Ohhh!" My fingers curl against his shoulders and seemingly of their own accord, my thighs lift up and clamp closed around his hips. My heart pounds; my head throbs. Every pull of his lips drags a long cry out of me, until I'm so breathless that it comes out as whimpers.

He wraps his arms around me firmly, pinning me down with his weight, and starts sucking harder. I moan encouragement, my hips shimmying against him by reflex as the heat between my thighs gets stoked higher and higher. "Don't stop...it's good...oh God it's so good," I sob.

The wildness in my head won't go away. I wail and shudder when he turns his attention to my other breast and then I gasp as he slides his hand between my thighs. He presses the heel of his hand against my aching pussy, then starts to massage it, sending slow waves of pleasure through my clit.

. . .

Holy shit! My eyes fly open, mouth falling open into an 'O' of shock, and my head dropping back as I start floating higher and higher on the mounting sensations. I'm staring up through the skylight at the stars as he keeps working on me, and my eyesight is starting to blur.

The bulge brushing against my thigh feels like it's getting bigger by the second. He grunts softly against my skin when my writhing leg slides against it, and I feel little shudders go through him. They turn me on almost as much as what he's doing to me.

My heart feels like it's going to pound its way out of my chest. It's too much; I'm overwhelmed, almost frightened. I whimper and start to pull away, pushing at his shoulders, and he raises his head to look at me.

"Do you need to catch your breath?" he purrs, and I whimper and nod, a little ashamed. He smiles, slow and warm, and nods. "Then let's get rid of those clothes."

The brief reprieve helps my heart slow down as he moves back and pulls my track pants off. Underneath I'm in another running thong, this one white. I noticed his reaction to the last one, and they're all I've been wearing ever since. His eyes light up as his gaze falls to the little triangle of fabric, now soaked with my juices and sticking to me.

I help kick off my pants, leaving only the thong, and I shudder with fresh desire as I see him straighten and stare at me hungrily. For a moment I think he's going to shuck off his underwear and mount me right there and then. He's already shown ten times the patience of any guy who's ever chased after me.

To MY SURPRISE, instead of climbing back over me, he takes me by the hips and pushes me back toward the curved headboard, sliding me up against a pile of pillows. Sliding forward, Damon shoulders my thighs apart, gently but insistently, and then crouches between them. His big hands cup my ass, squeezing and stroking...and then he lifts me to his mouth as he bends his face toward me.

I FEEL warm breath through the damp cloth and let out a long, crooning groan. He starts kissing my pussy through the fabric, smelling me, nuzzling me, as low rumbles of contentment escape him.

I PUSH up on my heels, squirming with excitement as he nibbles lightly over the barely-hidden curves of my pussy. Not long after, he's hooking a thumb in the straps on either side of my wet mound and tugging the fabric down.

THERE'S A MOMENT—JUST a moment—where my impatience to be free of clothing fights against the sudden shock of being naked in front of a man for the first time. I dig my fingers into the bedding and squeeze my eyes shut, forcing myself to keep from freezing up as I feel the fabric slide down my thighs and get pulled off over my feet. Then it's done—and I feel his hot breath on my bare skin as he bends to me.

. . .

I GASP and arch as his lips brush mine—the ones no man has ever touched—and then darts his tongue between my folds to explore. My fingertips feel like they're going to pop through the mattress upholstery as he starts lashing and swirling his tongue, teasing his way upward slowly toward my clit. The anticipation makes me ache.

THIS IS BETTER than any adolescent fantasy or heated daydream. Sensations I have never felt before run through my body, leaving me wet and trembling, my voice reduced to sobbing, half-coherent pleas. "Don't stop...please don't stop..."

FINALLY HIS TONGUE reaches my clit and starts flicking it delicately, even as one hand slides from my ass cheek and slips a single long finger into my aching cunt. I squeal with pleasure, clenching around it; another finger slips in beside it, opening me a little further.

TIME SEEMS TO DILATE, leaving me hanging somewhere between absolute bliss and desperate need. I can hear my cries echoing off the windows as his lashing tongue speeds up, and a third finger slips into me, stretching me further. I can't focus on anything but that long, soaring climb toward an even greater pleasure.

I'M STILL BEGGING, breathlessly now, the syllables coming randomly between desperate gasps. I feel my muscles tighten—and then he takes me that last inch into ecstasy.

. . .

I go wild, grinding and shaking against his face as he holds me firmly to the mattress. My mind goes blank; inside, I soar up like a firework and explode in pure, shameless joy. I can hear myself screaming, and even the faint pain in my throat feels good.

As I float back to Earth, my fragmented mind gathering back together peacefully, all I can think is, *so that's what I was missing,* along with the touch of the man of my dreams, anyway. I croon with pleasure as I feel him slide his fingers out of me and raise his lips from my tingling pussy.

"So good," I whisper.

"I'm not done with you," he rasps in a voice thick with lust. He wipes his mouth on the back of his arm and then climbs over me, pulling me into his arms.

I hold him, running my hands over the taut muscles of his back and then sliding them down over his ass. "I sure hope not," I pant softly, and then grip the waistband of his boxer briefs.

His eyes widen slightly and then narrow with pleasure as I tug the fabric down over his sculpted ass and slim hips. He grunts softly as I free his cock; I feel the smooth shaft slide against my hand briefly as the elastic clears the top of his thighs. Then he's parting my thighs again with his hands, and settling between them eagerly.

. . .

I feel the push of his cock and lift my hips invitingly; I'm so wet and relaxed that the tapered head slides into me right away. As he eases his way further inside me, though, I have to keep from tensing; his shaft is thick, and it stretches me open almost painfully.

He tosses his head, eyes narrowing to slits, his lips parting as he braces himself on his hands and pushes into me slowly. We both groan; I grab his ass and breathe deep, then arch up against him, encouraging.

He starts to thrust, and it hurts only a little; his slow caution has made sure I can take him without pain. He moans softly with each movement of his hips, his breath shuddering as his weight and his thrusts push me into the mattress deep enough to make the bedsprings creak. It feels incredible to be filled by him; I feel my excitement growing even before he shudders and starts getting a little rough.

His face is transformed by pleasure, all sternness gone, but his eyes are soft and bright as he gazes down at me. I beam, moving my body to meet his as I hold him in my arms. It's everything I had ever hoped for and more, and I feel a second orgasm start to build in me as his tremors grow more and more violent.

"Amy," he whispers, almost reverently—and then surprises me by slowing down.

I look up at him, at his taut muscles gleaming with sweat, his expression feverish with lust and need, and my own excitement only ebbs off a little. "What is it?" I breathe.

He smiles. "I want to watch you come again. With my cock inside of you this time."

He slides his hand out from under me and lays it just over my aching clit, and then starts rubbing and kneading me as he holds still inside of me. The whole time, he's watching my face.

I let out a soft gasp and squirm under him, feeling my body begin ramping up fast toward another climax. This time, it's more peaceful; I know what is coming, and I crave it, instead of feeling overwhelmed. "Yes," I whisper. "Yes, yes, *yes*..."

It happens again, the waves of sensation exploding outward from my clit as I thrash and grind under him. He stiffens—and then his loud groan drowns me out as his cock starts to pulse and twitch.

For one long, glorious moment, we stretch against each other, holding on hard as he spills deep inside of me. Then the last spasm passes and we collapse, tangled together on the mattress.

I don't realize I've blacked out until I open my eyes to discover myself nestled in his arms, the breeze from the ceiling fan cooling my body. My leg feels a little sore, my inner thighs as well, and every muscle in my body is completely loose. *Wow*, I think, lying still for a few moments as I get my bearings.

. . .

MY CHEEK IS PILLOWED on his upper arm, and he's curled around me from behind, kissing my shoulder and the back of my neck now and again. He senses the change in my breathing, and he murmurs, "Are you all right?" in my ear.

I smile lazily and stretch, feeling my joints pop and a tingle run through my body. I feel his cock stir against my back, and my smile widens. "Never better," I murmur.

THEN I ROLL over and reach for him again.

CHAPTER 8

Damon

For a long time, Amy and I can't let each other go. Now that I know there's no point in trying to hold back, I'm committed. I lose track of the number of times we make love that night.

I haven't been this eager since I was a teen. I have far more strength and skill now, and more self-control, too, but my desire for her burns so hot that I wear us both out by the time it cools enough to let me rest. Finally, we end up collapsed in a limp tangle again, with me sprawled out and her curled on my chest, dozing.

For the first time in my life, the peace that I only feel after orgasm follows me into sleep, and it's there still when I wake perhaps an hour later. It only deepens as I reach for Amy again. The weight of the past is lifting away, leaving me with a glimpse of a future that is richer and kinder than the isolation and endless patrolling I've been living through for the past decade.

SHE TREMBLES under me as I move slowly against her, savoring each embrace of my cock by her swollen, slick pussy. Her muscles tighten around me and she lets out that sweet little moan again, and I gently rub her clit until it becomes a long, cooing cry. Her muscles ripple over me, and I suck air through my teeth, fighting to last.

THE LOOK of amazement on her face each time she settles down from climax tells me so much. As do the quiet, happy tears I kiss off her cheeks. She's been lonely and frustrated as hell too.

AND AS FOR THE REST...HAVING had to ease her into taking my cock and having heard her screams of amazement the first time I brought her to climax, I'm not all that surprised when she finally admits, "I've never done this before."

But the next part is a surprise. "I've never wanted to with anyone else."

IT HITS hard as the full implication dawns. I stare down at her, still buried in her flesh, my body taut with excitement but my mind already rejoicing. "Never?"

"THEY WEREN'T YOU," she breathes as I feel my loins tighten

dangerously. She sees the look on my face, and her tender smile turns a little naughty. Her hips start to roll softly under me, sending growing swells of pleasure up my shaft. "You ruined me for other men before you ever touched me."

It's too much. I thrust deep into her, pushing her into the mattress, and my back arches with pleasure. I hear her whispering soft endearments in my ear, though my hoarse groans almost drown her out...and then her whispers break up into soft gasps as my frantic grinding makes her soar with me.

This time, I don't fight to hold it at bay; as she digs her nails into my back and shudders with bliss, I come so hard that I scream.

I barely catch my weight once the climax burns through my strength; she sighs and wraps her arms around me as I settle over her, my whole body tingling and refusing to move. She purrs and stretches under me, sending a fresh shudder of pleasure through me.

"Stay here," she murmurs in my ear. "Stay inside me."

I do, too content to argue that I must be crushing her. I doze, satiated and at peace, head on her shoulder, feeling her fingers combing through my hair until they slow and settle as she drops off to sleep. I relax, barely noticing when my own eyes close firmly.

. . .

MEMORIES RUSH OVER ME: Mirror Lake at dawn when I was a kid; the Great Erg covered with a dusting of snow; Amazonian otters the size of wolves; the flowered slopes of the Kabul hills after a rain. A whole world of beauty and wonder that my mind absorbed in passing, but that made so little impression on my heart when I was there.

BACK THEN, traveling the globe as a soldier for hire, I was too focused on survival, and then on profit—and then, on getting out—to notice much. Now, the memories I built around my career—the people, the places, the natural beauty—come back to me, and with them, a sense of regret. I have been caught in a holding pattern, obsessively trying to protect one place while a whole world waits out there to enjoy.

I SUDDENLY FEEL nostalgic and wake up with the overwhelming urge to go back—and with the overwhelming scent of Amy in my nose, my face nestled in her hair. I want to go...and I want to take her with me. For keeps.

I LIE THERE, entwined with her, watching her sleep as I sort out what's in my head.

I LOVE her enough to know she deserves a better man than I have ever been. But she loves me, and it hurts her when I try to keep her at arm's length. I can't do that anymore.

· · ·

So I have to try and be the man she believes I am...for the rest of my life, if she'll have me.

I fall asleep, this time feeling more contentment than I ever have in my life.

I wake up confused; her warm presence in the bed is gone. "Amy?" I turn my head, looking around for her.

Her clothes are gone. No noise from the bathroom. *She's just downstairs somewhere,* I try to reassure myself as my stomach tightens, and I slip out of bed.

She could be exploring the tower, which she's clearly fascinated by. She could be out for a walk; it's morning, after all. It could be any one of dozens of completely ordinary things that will see her returning to me soon.

But the cold finger of fear won't leave the back of my neck as I yank on my boxer briefs and make my way out of the bedroom to look for her. "Amy? I'm awake. Would you like some breakfast?"

No answer. I can't help the growing tension gathering in my body as I pad around the tower, searching every room, looking out every window.

. . .

NOT ON THE UPPER FLOORS. Not in the garden. I finally reach my second-floor den and discover the television on and tuned to the local news station.

"AMY?" Not here. But she left so quickly that she left the television on. That is not a good sign.

I FOCUS on the news report, trying to figure out what might have sent her fleeing without so much as waking me to say goodbye. A recap of the last hour comes on...and I shudder, my eyes widening. *Fuck.*

"NINETEEN-YEAR-OLD CHAD EVANSTON was found shot dead this morning, the culmination of a two-day crime spree for which he was the prime suspect and assumed ringleader. It's not yet known who shot Chad or under what circumstances. But after attacks on three different women and girls and an act of arson and vandalism that destroyed two automobiles, police suspect that Evanston's last intended victim, whoever she was, may have been armed."

I STARE at the television as bits of story they've built so far unfold. I know that I didn't shoot Evanston. So should Amy. After all, while Chad was dying, she and I were here, safe in the tower, making love.

But it's still one hell of a coincidence, and she doesn't know whether I have any other operatives. I don't, but...

GODDAMN IT. My heart sinks into my shoes.

SOMEONE HAS JUST MURDERED Chad Evanston, and in the court of Amy's trust, I'm the prime suspect. *I knew this couldn't last,* I think, fighting a surge of anguish.

BUT THEN I take a deep breath, and lift my head. *No. Someone killed Chad last night. It wasn't me, and I'll prove it to her somehow.*

I'M NOT GIVING her up without a fight, now that I have her. No fucking way.

CHAPTER 9

Amy

"You said you were done with killing!" I sob into the phone. I'm more disappointed than I ever thought I could be in my life. I know that I can't possibly trust Damon now—or ever, unless he proves pretty damn quick that my fears are unfounded.

It's been the better part of a day, and the Sheriff's Department is no closer to catching a suspect. Fear that Damon is going to be the one led away in handcuffs is only one of my many agonizing worries; they've left me pacing and sick, filled with betrayed anger.

"Amy...darling," Damon's voice is gentle but holds a touch of strain, "I didn't kill Evanston. I was with you all yesterday afternoon and last night. You know where all my strength and focus was—it was on you. I couldn't possibly have shot him."

I CLOSE MY EYES, feeling some of my outrage ebb away. *He was with me. One hundred percent with me. When we stopped making love, it was only because we both needed rest, not because he had to leave.*

HE COULD HAVE SENT someone to kill the bastard with one phone call, though.

"LOOK...I..." What he says makes sense, except that this is a guy who has every creep and asshole in town terrified of him. And they're not scared for nothing. "Well, what the fuck happened, then?" I demand.

"I DON'T KNOW YET. But I'm going to find out. I send people to jail, Amy, and I scare them out of town. At worst I might smack some particularly violent idiot around. I *don't* leave some kid's corpse lying in the middle of the street for the poor mail carrier to find."

He takes a huge breath. "Please. Give me a chance to prove myself to you. You said you believed in me."

MY EYES STING SUDDENLY. I want to go running back into his arms even if he did shoot that little shit. But I need to know that I can trust him. "And you warned me not to," I say very softly.

. . .

"And I was fucking stupid to do that, Amy. I was trying to keep you at arm's length because I figured you'd be too horrified by my past to deal with me. But it is still my *past*, Amy. I don't kill any more. It would have to be life or death with no choice at all before I'd do that again."

His tone is both solemn and pleading, and it hurts to hear it. I never in my life believed that the Guardian could be vulnerable because of me. But loneliness can be the chink in anyone's armor.

"I love you," I say softly and hear him catch his breath. "I couldn't change that if I wanted to. But I have to know that that part of you is in the past. ...That I can trust you."

"I'll prove it." His voice drops to a resolute growl.

"How do you plan to do that?" I wonder aloud. He sounds a little like he might already be onto something, which weakens my suspicion even more.

"I'm taking you with me to find this guy. You're going to be in on every step of investigation, every interview, every bit of what I do to clear my name for you."

The determination in his voice only grows...and I have to admit, it's catching. I can't listen to it and not believe—at least a little—that he's going to come through for me.

I HESITATE. I used to daydream about being his superhero sidekick back when I was twelve. Now the Guardian wants to take me on an investigation for real...and the outcome will determine whether we stay together or part ways.

THERE'S part of me that still wants to tell him to go fuck himself. How many people could there be in this tiny town that are capable of shooting someone? Could it be more than one? And why?

I'M SO USED to people disappointing me that it's almost instinct to distrust Damon. But in all my life, he's the only one who *hasn't* disappointed me—up until this point. My gut is at war with itself, trying to figure out the truth. But I have to give him a chance.

"ALL RIGHT," I say finally, praying that I'm making the right call. "I'll give this a shot for you. Don't disappoint me."

I MEAN it with all my heart. I endured the biggest letdown of my life this morning—even worse than realizing that my parents don't love me. Not because I learned Evanston was dead—I couldn't shed a tear for that piece of garbage if I tried—but because I thought Damon had lied to me about something that important.

. . .

I can't go through that again. And I'm taking that risk by trusting him with any kind of second chance. "Swear," I murmur.

"I swear that I won't disappoint you," he replies in that solemn tone, but I can hear the faint thread of relief behind it.

"You had better not. Because I can forgive your past, but I won't forgive bullshit. I've choked on enough of that in my life." It's weird using his own Scary Voice back at him, but it's certainly warranted.

His voice warms a little. "I understand."

We sign off, and I hang up to get ready. I rented the last room in the cheapest bed and breakfast in town, and I putter around the small space putting together an outfit that doesn't have grass stains on it. I settle for black jeans and a black tank top, and then I braid my hair to keep it out of my eyes.

My leg feels fine now that I've had a walk and some more rest. It helps that I have a touch of hope. I'm angry, I'm hurt, and I'm still remembering how my heart felt like it was being ripped in half when I heard about Evanston being gunned down in the street...but Damon has some things in his favor.

One, I really am his alibi, unless he sent someone else. And two, if Damon had killed someone, he wouldn't have left an incriminating corpse lying around, would he?

THERE'S something else that haunts me as I get ready to meet up with Damon. Something that I can't ignore. How close did I come, in defense of my life, to looping my bag strap around a boy's neck that night and squeezing?

IF SOMEONE HURT Damon like that, would I want him dead? Could I blame Damon for wanting him dead? Maybe not—but he swore to me that he's done with that life.

ON MY WAY OUT, I decide to hide my eyes with dark sunglasses. I don't want Damon to see how much I've been crying.

WHEN I SEE HIM, I stop in my tracks on the stairs of the bed and breakfast, frozen as a frightened deer. He's standing there in a new leather shirt, gray jeans and combat boots, eyes covered by sunglasses—all business. Just looking at him turns me on, as if knowing what pleasures he can give me has made him that much more irresistible.

BUT I CAN'T AFFORD to give in to those feelings. I can't afford to do what I want and run down the stairs to embrace him. I have given him this one chance to prove once and for all that I can trust him to keep his bloody past in the past. It doesn't mean everything suddenly goes back to normal.

. . .

"We'll go to see the deputy first," he tells me as he waits for me. The sound of his voice—solemn and full of strength—reminds me of what we're fighting for today. I nod and get moving, walking down to join him on the sidewalk. "The county coroner will have sent him a report by now."

"Is he going to have a problem with me being there?" I ask, tilting my head to look up at him. We still haven't touched.

He nods and opens the door for me. "Good point. I'll explain things."

He glances at me now and again as he drives us over. "You've been following the story on the town website?" he finally asks as we get near the station at the far end of town.

"Yes. They're still looking for witnesses." I look up at him. "They're looking for the other three boys too."

"They've probably left town." He scowls. "If they weren't such rank amateurs, I would suspect that one of them killed Evanston, because he was the only one who showed his face. We'll just have to see who goes missing in the next week or so."

His voice is very calm and controlled. It contains almost none of last night's warmth. His emotional armor is at full strength, and it hurts to feel locked out from him.

. . .

Then again, he's probably feeling about the same way about me. "I guess you're right. I just wish we had seen their faces too." I feel a chill run down my back as I think about it.

I DON'T KNOW who tried to get me into that van that night. I don't know who put a bullet in both Evanston and my new relationship with one pull of the trigger. I'm sick to death of all these unknowns!

"Me, too, sweetheart," he says with real regret. It takes everything I can do not to lay a hand on his thigh as he drives, but I'm still wary, so I keep my hand to myself.

The town deputy is a sweet-faced, chubby redhead who looks like a very large Boy Scout. He shakes hands with Damon and gives me a slightly confused smile. "Amy was the second attempted kidnapping victim the night of the crime spree," Damon says smoothly, and he bobs his head, seeming to understand.

"Well, the coroner says it was a small caliber bullet fired at close range, though not point-blank. It severed the spine at the first cervical vertebra and exited through the face." He pushes a sheaf of papers across his desk with thick fingers, and Damon takes them, turning them and spreading them so I can look at their contents too.

. . .

I've never read a coroner's report before. But one thing stands out for me. "If this person fired at an upward angle, doesn't that mean that they would have to be shorter than Evanston?"

Damon's eyes light up. "Good catch. According to the report, the way that he fell indicates that he was shot while walking upright, by someone who came up behind him. That person could only fire upward if they were shorter or crouching and that would cause powder burns to the face."

I look at his smooth cheeks and chin, and feel another touch of relief. No burns there. *Is this all a misunderstanding?*

"There can't be too many guys in town shorter than five foot ten who also own a gun," Deputy Metcalf muses. "Maybe one of the dads of the victims could have done it, but chances are that whoever did this was a woman."

"If it was self-defense, though, she wouldn't have snuck up and shot him from behind." Damon strokes his chin. "Maybe revenge for an attack?"

"When we get the ballistics reports, we'll know more. The gun might actually be registered. This isn't the big city, after all. It's not so easy to get an unregistered gun." Metcalf exchanged glances with Damon, then looked at me again. "You all right, miss?"

I'm missing something important. Even as the relief of understanding that Damon's very likely too damn tall to be the killer washes over me, I feel a sudden wave of nausea come right on its tail. *One of the fathers...*

"I have four pistols registered. Do you want me to turn any of them in for testing?" Damon is asking.

The deputy gives him a shrewd look. "You have any .22 caliber pistols?"

He scoffs. "You know I don't go in for that wimpy shit."

"Well, the killer did. There was also bits of down found in the wound. Whoever did this slipped up behind the guy with a pillow or folded piece of down clothing and fired through it with a low caliber piece to make the kill as quiet as possible." Deputy Metcalf points out one of the ultrasound images.

I can't speak yet, but I'm feeling sicker and sicker.

"An amateur assassin," Damon says slowly.

"A coward," I choke out. He turns to look at me and frowns with concern.

"Amy, what is it?"

. . .

I LOOK between the two of them with tears in my eyes, feeling ice in my veins on this warm night. "I know who killed Evanston."

I DO, and I wish I didn't. I know what telling them will lead to. But as I tell them anyway, and their expressions go from curious to stunned to grim, I know what has to be done.

CHAPTER 10

Damon

We arrest the killer half an hour later at his home. His wife screams bloody murder about it until the Deputy threatens her with charges for obstruction. Then, she has nothing to say at all.

I keep a supportive arm around Amy as they bring her father out in handcuffs. The strange, alarming little man has no expression on his face; his eyes are dull, his skin colorless, and his manner almost dazed. He does not look at his daughter as he walks by.

"I know you didn't do this to avenge what those boys tried to do to me," Amy calls out suddenly from the shelter of my arm. Her voice is hard and cold, and I recognize my own cadence in it again. "So why the hell did you do it, you cowardly old monster?"

Her father stops suddenly and looks slowly up at her. He seems puzzled as if the answer should be obvious. "He burned my car," he says simply with no emotion in his voice.

"It could have been anything," she says breathlessly as we drive back to the tower. There's no question now that she believes my innocence; she found the real killer herself. "Anything at all could have set him off. Including me staying at his house too long."

I don't know what to say to this. One of the mistakes of my past was assuming she would be better off with her biological family. She says she forgives me and that she wants to focus on the future instead of the past. But right now, she's dealing with something horrifying.

"He purchased the murder weapon a week ago for home defense." I shudder, imagining him using the excuse of a mistake or accident to shoot his own daughter one night as she came in the door. I know she's thinking the same.

"If you hadn't taken me in, it could have been me instead of Evanston," she mumbles.

"Sweetheart...maybe. But what-ifs will do your head in. The point is, that's not what happened. It's okay now," I tell her softly.

She swallows, tears in her eyes. "Yes. I just...I'm wondering how many times you're going to end up saving me."

"As many times as it takes to make sure you're safe and happy," I promise, and I don't care if it makes me sound soft.

Her smile is like the sun breaking through the clouds. I smile back and turn onto my private drive. Almost home.

CHAPTER 11

Amy

"So what did the doctor say?" Damon asks as I walk out into the waiting room. He stands up as I walk to him and pulls me into his arms; I lay my cheek against his broad chest and feel his heart beat through the thin silk of his shirt.

"I'm cleared to return by fall semester," I say cheerfully as he strokes my back. An old lady across the waiting room gives us a disapproving stare; I smile back happily until she looks away. "Are you sure you want to join me in Denver for the year?"

He flashes a grin. "Absolutely. The Butte can look after itself for a few months."

He takes my hand, thumb brushing briefly over the slim rose gold engagement ring he put on it a week ago. So much can change in just a month.

And it's not just our relationship that's changed, either. My father remains in jail; my mother is filing for divorce. She tried to call me once for support, and I slowly hung up the phone on her.

I don't know if I can ever forgive her for siding against me with that monster she called a husband for so many years. Maybe someday. But for now, she'll have to fend for herself, just as she decided that I should.

The Evanstons and three other families moved out of town in the wake of the shooting. It seems really ironic that the parents of those little rapists would do so much to protect them, when I've done nothing, and mine would never protect me.

But the parents you get are the luck of the draw. Now friends and lovers, those are the people that you can choose. I know I've chosen well, just as my mother once chose poorly.

"I was thinking of doing some traveling during winter break," he says breezily, offering me a better future with every plan he makes. "Have you ever been to Brazil?"

"No, but I've always wanted to go," I reply, my smile widening a little.

"Well then," the Guardian says happily as we return to our home. "Let's make some plans to fix that."

The End.

SIGN UP TO RECEIVE FREE BOOKS

Sign Up to Receive Free E-Books and Audiobook Codes.

Would you like to read **The Unexpected Nanny, Dirty Little Virgin** and **other romance books** for **free**?

You can sign up to receive these free e-books and audiobooks by typing this link into your browser:

https://www.steamyromance.info/free-books-and-audiobooks-hot-and-steamy/

Or this one:

https://www.steamyromance.info/the-unexpected-nanny-free/

PREVIEW OF THE MOUNTAIN MAN'S SECRET

AN OLDER MAN YOUNGER WOMAN ROMANCE

"The Mountain Man's Secret"
"Twice Her Hero"
"The City Girl's Protector"
"The Blizzard"
Christmas Eve Showdown", and "A Hero for Christmas"

(Older Man/Younger Woman, Criminal/Outlaw, Virgin/Never Had an Orgasm, Christmas, and Secret Baby.)

By Michelle Love

∼

Blurb

I came to the mountains after my old partners murdered my wife.

I'm safe here and self-sufficient—but alone.
Then I find Belle: stranded in a snowstorm and about to die.

I save her life and take her home.
She's lonely; so am I.
We band together so we don't have to face the holiday season alone.
Nature takes its course; now a baby's coming.
But so are my ex-partners.
I'm not running this time.
And they're not taking my woman from me again.

When a sudden snowstorm strands her on a back road in the New York Catskill Mountains, Belle is rescued by a hot local mountain man with a dark secret. Carl is a former bank robber who has holed up on family land after an ex-partner murders his girlfriend to keep her quiet. After ratting on his partner for the slaying, Carl hides in his mountain survivalist fortress to avoid the police and his old cronies. By confiding in her gossipy obstetrician, Belle inadvertently alerts the gang to Carl's whereabouts. Knowing they can't attack the man in his fortress of a home, they surround the hotel where Belle stays when she's not with him and threaten to burn it down if he will not turn himself in. The lovers must work together to battle his old partners and protect themselves and their child.

CHAPTER 1

Belle

"You're kidding me," I stare at the white-out conditions whirling around my car. The aging beige subcompact that negotiates the streets of Poughkeepsie so well is no match for the Catskills in winter. Unfortunately, I've discovered that way too late.

I started the day packing and handing off my apartment keys to my subleaser, bubbling over with excitement and impatient to get going. Ever since winning the state arts grant to produce my photo book on Catskill wildlife in winter, I've been over the moon. I'm thrilled to finally land a paid project where I can show off my talents as well as remind my fellow New Yorkers about the importance of conservation.

It means giving up Thanksgiving and Christmas to the project. But I was going to spend them alone anyway. The venture gives me a good reason to be alone, fills my time, and gives me something to look forward to this coming Christmas season despite my isolation.

Amazing that only half an hour ago, loneliness at Christmas was my biggest problem.

I had packed for fall, for a Poughkeepsie autumn, along with a good pair of hiking boots. Twenty minutes ago, it *was* Fall, the trees still full of gold and crimson and brown leaves. Twenty minutes ago, I was still thinking the same stupid things that brought me up here unprepared.

So what if I've never been to the Catskills in winter? It's mid November—chances are there won't even be snow on the ground until December. Besides, I'm an experienced hiker—how much tougher could it be to cross the same terrain with snow on the ground?

I look out the side window at the narrow valley that creeps between the toes of the mountain. The snow is turning everything alien, blurring the outlines of the rocky slope and covering the trees with clots of white. It's not idyllic; it's not pretty; I stare at it and feel dread tighten my guts.

"Yeah, you thought it all out, Belle. But now here you are: maybe an hour away from becoming a popsicle. Good job." My voice shakes as the snow piles up on the windshield.

Apparently New York weather doesn't give a damn about keeping to its proper season. I've been coming up here for years; I should have figured this out. Except I'm originally from Miami; winter is unfamiliar to me. During my first winter here, I barely left my apartment for three full months.

Excited at my big chance, I forgot my common sense. What is going on? How far has my holiday depression put me that I end up like this?

It was all right when the storm hit. I kept control of the car, even in the gusty swirling wind, and managed to stay on the road when visibility cut to almost nothing in less than a minute.

I wasn't okay out here, and I pulled over to shelter from the wind against the mountainside.

And then my engine died.

And didn't want to start again.

I'm too pissed to be completely terrified yet. *Belle Evans, aspiring photographer, found dead in her car on the side of Mount Tremper. According to the preliminary report from rescue workers, the cause of death was terminal stupidity.*

"Stop that," I mutter as the wind rocks my car again. "You're not dead yet."

I keep thinking I'll get lucky. Someone will come along in a car, or better yet, a truck with a tow hook and a plow. This is a state highway, even if it's in the middle of bumble-ass nowhere.

What if I'm wrong? People really die here. Once the battery dies and the heater goes off... And the battery will die even faster in these cold temps.

And the horn is useless. Unlike most New Yorkers, I rarely use my car horn much, so when it broke, it never occurred to me to replace it. I regret that now; although, there's no guarantee anyone could hear a car horn over the roaring wind.

I start to shiver, even though the heater's still blasting. *Is it worth the risk to get out of the car and look for help?*

Probably not. The last sign said five miles to the nearest town. I can't walk five miles in this; even if I don't wander off the road in the white-out, I'll likely end up with hypothermia.

I'm trapped. I really am going to die up here alone! Nobody will get to me in time!

I clench my fists, forcing them to still. *Stop thinking like this!* If I'm going to die, I should fight right up to when the lights go out. Scaring myself will just drain away the energy I need.

I pull out my phone and try calling for help. It won't connect; zero bars. *Crap! Well, my garbage luck is holding.*

Pain and frustration squeeze my heart. I can't even call my mom to get advice or comfort. Or to say goodbye, for that matter.

Mom. She's down in Miami, far from where she can help, and she may not know for over a week that her stupid daughter froze to death in a snow bank. *She never wanted me to move north in the first place...*

That's the fatal thought; I start crying, a deep grief filling me.

I sob so hard I feel like throwing up; my head pounds, my eyes sting, and for a few moments the wind is silenced. I try again to get the engine to turn over; it rattles and clunks and then dies with a shudder. I let out a scream and pound the steering wheel once with the side of my fist.

The pain of that impact shocks me partway back to myself. I wipe my cheeks and squeeze my eyes shut. "Stop it. Stop it now. You won't save yourself by sitting here crying."

What to do? Think! The wind shakes the car again, and I let out a cry of consternation, but then buckle down. *No time to be scared.*

Conserve energy. I turn off the dome light and the headlights, leaving only my emergency blinkers on and the heater running.

Bundle up. I turn and reach into the backseat of my car, grabbing and dragging my duffel bag up into the passenger seat. On go more sweaters, my coat, and a purple beanie, pulled down low over my ears.

More socks on my feet. Two pairs on my hands. The empty duffel bag blanketed over me. I feel like a laundry pile with a face but it's so warm with the heater going that I start to sweat.

I turn it down. The idea is to protect me from hypothermia, not make me sweat through all my clothes. Besides, this way the battery will last longer.

I lay back in my seat, watching the hole in the piled-up snow slowly get smaller and smaller on the windshield until my view is blocked entirely. Still no sign of another car. I have to stop myself from getting worked up.

Calm. Stay calm. Someone will come.

The heater fan stutters; the dashboard lights flicker. The battery is dying. I yank off the socks and gloves on my hands and pull out my phone again to look at it once more. One single bar —I can call for help!

Nothing.

A moment later, the power shuts off entirely.

I let out a high, startled cry before clamping my hand over my mouth. *That won't help.* I shudder, tears running down my cheeks, but my mind slowly clears.

I close my eyes, doing my best not to panic. Waiting is the only thing to do. I have no flares or emergency radio; I could get out and look for a better phone signal to call for help, but how fast will I freeze through if I try?

Besides, opening the door will let all the heat out. Better to wait until it's completely cold in here. Maybe the snow will stop in the meantime.

So I wait. And the temperature drops. And the storm keeps raging.

Fighting my fear again, my shivering breath is visible. Tears streak down to sting my chilled cheeks. I grit my teeth and pull the collars of my sweaters and coat over my face until only my eyes peek out.

Be strong, Belle.

Except it just keeps getting colder!

Finally I shiver so hard that I'm convinced it must be just as cold outside. Even with the socks on them, my fingers are numb.

My dread mounts as the lack of sensation builds in my toes and creeps slowly up my fingers. I shake my hands out, slapping them against my thighs, and stomp my boots. Agonizing pins and needles begin spreading through my hands and feet; I stuff the sock-wrapped bundles of my hands under my arms and tuck my legs.

"I'm not giving up," I rasp in a snuffled voice dripping with terror. As my fingers and toes burn with pain, the fear just keeps mounting.

Just at that moment, when I can't bear any more, a sound pierces my awareness between the thundering gusts of wind. I hear a high growl of an engine like a dirt bike...or a snowmobile. It's coming up the road!

"Oh, thank God." As the engine noise grows louder and closer, I realize I'm thoroughly tangled up in all this cloth, and I struggle with it, swearing and flailing.

"Don't pass by!" I shout, fumbling my arm free and reaching for the door.

Whoever is on the snowmobile slows down and pulls up alongside the car. A faint glare of a headlamp is distinguishable through the accumulated snow.

A moment later, a huge shadow falls across my side window and someone knocks on it.

Sobbing with relief, I shuffle the socks off my hands and reach for the latch.

CHAPTER 2

Carl

"I hate freak storms," I mutter into my helmet steering the snowmobile down the mountain slope. It's not that they're inconvenient, they're also deadly.

The snow pelts my back and sides as I drive. I'm cautious, slowing through the thicker areas to avoid getting blown into a tree. A bundle of emergency gear strapped to the back of the snowmobile jostles as I make turns.

This damn storm will catch some people. Every time tourists come up here, which is ten months out of the year, trouble ensues. They don't know the Catskills; they don't know how to read the sky.

And since some of those tourists will die otherwise, I go deal with it.

I've been living here for five years, mostly off of what I hunt, fish, breed, keep, trap, and gather. I don't even go into town if I can help it. Today, I will probably have to.

I knew the damn storm was approaching two hours ago. I saw it in the gunmetal clouds and felt it in the icy bite of the wind. When the blizzard hit—and this is a straight up blizzard—my place was already battened down with the rooster, goats, and hens safely inside.

Now, I have to bundle up and go out in this mess again. Not looking forward to it. If I stay by my wood stove all lazy and cozy, they'll find frozen bodies along the highway by tomorrow morning.

I remember the first time I found one. It's why I started going out every time we have an unexpected storm. That was the March Blizzard of 2016; it stranded snow bunnies up at the lodge and caused fifteen car accidents and six deaths.

I found the sixth one. The poor girl was barely old enough to drive. She panicked and left her car in the middle of the storm looking for help after running it deep into a snow bank.

She was dressed in club wear and on her way down from the mountain resort. She had a coat on, but her legs were bare, feet in tottery heels, and fishnet gloves frozen to her skin. I found her in the snow curled into a ball, her face hidden under the collar of her jacket.

Her name was Anna Crenshaw. And ever since then, in her memory, I have gone out into the snow with warming blankets and heat packs, looking for the possible casualties.

Right now, I'm very cautiously driving the snowmobile through this mess. The roaring wind and the sting of snow against the bridge of my nose are unpleasant, but they keep me alert. Cold dulls your senses; I don't want to miss anything. Or anyone.

No more funerals for people I could have saved.

Driving alongside the road and sometimes on it, the snow is so thick that the snowmobile never bottoms out. Eventually, the road starts running cliffside, and I simply drive down it, keeping my eyes peeled for stalled cars, people walking...crumpled figures.

I find two people in a stalled car in the first half hour of the storm. I help get them down to town and start my search again. No other abandoned cars for another ten miles, and I wonder if I got lucky.

Then, just as I'm thinking of stopping for a breather and a hot cup of coffee, another stranded car on the shoulder gets my attention. It looks like a compact: too small to be out here. It's coated in snow, and there's a dangerous snow load on the cliff-side overhang directly above it.

A slow, ugly creak sounds from the snow bank crowning the overhang. A thick gout of powder drips from its base where it casts its shadow over the car. The car's about to get buried—and possibly smashed in the process!

Someone might still be in there!

I speed up, coming alongside the vehicle and immediately start banging on the side window. For a moment, there's no response. Then a rustle and someone struggles with the door latch. The grunts and cries of distress and effort are high-pitched: it's either a woman or a kid.

A few small chunks of snow drop from the overhang and burst into powder on the roof. Then another one, the size of a baseball, leaving a small dent before it breaks apart. I bang on the window again. "Get moving! There's an avalanche coming!"

The door opens and a bundle of clothes with flailing arms and legs spills out into the snow almost at my feet. A cry of distress again as they fight to get to their feet.

"Get on behind me!" I shout and then reach down to help lift the small stranger onto the back of the snowmobile.

The Bundle wraps its arms around me as far as they will go and squeaks something I can't make out. "Hang on!" I order, and I pray they are capable.

A chunk of snow the size of my head shatters right next to us and a shadow ominously covers the car. I hear a creak, and then a single sharp crack, and I gun my engine. We dart away—just in time.

Seconds later, the entire snow load on the overhang comes down hard, bursting into an overwhelming mountain of powder against the car, which groans, crunches, and spits tinkling glass and metal across the road. The stranger screams and clings harder to me as snow sprays us. Then it's over as I leave the disaster behind us.

Just down the road, I pull over to a rest stop and stop beneath the overhang. The Bundle utters tiny, whimpering breaths. I gently pry their koala-like grip off of me. "It's okay," I call above the wind. "You'll be all right."

I get off and turn to the figure, who sits unsteadily on the back of the snowmobile. The whimpering breaths continue. This is probably a woman; a woman's sounds of terror are dreadful.

"Look, it'll be okay. I'll take you into town. You can warm up and call someone." I reach out for the stranger's shoulder...

...and a moment later, I'm catching her as she pitches forward in a dead faint.

She's small and light; it's effortless to lift her, and I gently nudge her. "Hey! Don't check out on me here!"

She doesn't respond. I pull her collar down and see a young woman's pretty, unconscious face.

"...Shit."

CHAPTER 3

Belle

It's warm when I wake up. My fingers and toes can wiggle, my skin doesn't sting, my nipples aren't hard beads of pain. My heart's beating, and the air around me is faintly stuffy and smells of wood smoke.

I'm alive.
Someone came and pulled me out.

Tears of relief pool in my eyes and spill out; I gulp and sniffle and finally open an eye to take a look around. I'm not in a hotel or a hospital. I'm in a small, rustic space with heavily plastered walls.

The surface beneath the thin mattress I'm on is hard, but deep warmth radiates through it. I'm lying on a sort of broad adobe bench attached to a very odd-looking wood stove. It's topped with something that looks like an oil drum, and a teakettle is steaming away on top of it.

A chair creaks. "You're awake," rumbles a deep, rich voice behind me. I roll over and see the man from the snowmobile.

The memory of him floods my hazy mind: his banging on the window, me falling out of the car, him helping me onto the snowmobile and then driving away fast just before half the hillside came down on top of my car.

Now that he's shed his snowsuit and parka, he's just as enormous; he's so striking that for a few moments all I can do is stare. Despite his height, he's on the leaner side of muscular, like a man who works instead of works out. Long arms, big hands, broad shoulders.

Pale green eyes regard me thoughtfully, and I am captivated. Regardless of his build, his face is smooth, his dark brown hair and beard cropped neatly and close. His nose is a little sharp, and crow's feet are starting at the corners of his eyes, but if he's more than thirty-five I'll be really surprised.

He's dressed exactly as I would expect any mysterious mountain man would be: work boots, jeans, a few layers of flannel shirts with the sleeves rolled up to his elbows. I remember his confidence on the snowmobile...and also what he said.

"This isn't a hotel," I mumble, gazing at his face. My voice sounds thick and raspy.

He blinks, and then nods and sighs. "No, when you collapsed I figured you better go someplace warm. The town is five miles away. My place was only two."

I nod slowly, sitting up on my elbows. I'm sore in spots, but the deep relaxation of being truly warm makes it barely a nuisance. Mostly I'm just relieved...and curious. "Thank you for saving me. Who are you?"

He considers me for a moment as if weighing how much to tell. Finally, he just says, "Carl. I live up here."

I look around, frowning slightly. The room has a snug, well-insulated feel to it. There are only windows along one wall. It's dark outside; I must have been out for hours.

"Belle," I reply distractedly. "I didn't even know there was a house on this side of the mountain."

"Not on," he says as he walks over to pull on a silicone glove and grab the teakettle off the drum. Its whistle dies; he moves past the stove and out of sight. "In. This house is earth-sheltered. The south-facing exterior is all native stone and timber. Nobody can see it from the road." His voice is calm and frank.

"Oh. Okay. I'm only asking because this is the area I got permission to do my survey in." I sit up, gathering the slightly scratchy wool blanket around me as I draw my knees against my chest and look over.

He's at a table on the far side of the stove, making tea in two white-flecked blue steel cups. "Survey?" he asks with a lifted eyebrow. The delicate scent of jasmine tea mixes oddly but pleasantly with the wood smoke.

"Yeah, I'm a wildlife photographer. Earth-sheltered? This house is mostly underground? No wonder I'm so warm."

I lower my legs to the floor, noticing my clothes are folded and stacked neatly at the end of the odd bench. "Thank you for saving my life," I add belatedly.

He grunts acknowledgment but doesn't answer, instead he continues puttering with the tea. "Honey?" he asks after a moment.

"Um, please." Normally I wouldn't ruin jasmine tea with honey, but right now something sweet sounds perfect. "I'm sorry, is all of this your land or something? They didn't tell me anyone actually owned it."

"I keep a low profile and don't complain much if people want to hike along the ridgeline or whatever. It only comes up when people try to poach on my land or grab one of my livestock. Mostly I just go about my business and let others do the same."

He brings me the tea, holding it steady until I have a good grip on the hot metal.

I set it next to me, on the clay instead of the thin mattress. "Oh. If I had known I would have asked your permission."

He cocks an eyebrow. "You've got it, if you learn to keep out of trouble up here. Smart thinking with bundling up like that, but you don't seem like you spend much time Upstate."

"Not in the mountains, no, not in winter. I'm out of Poughkeepsie," I admit, feeling a blush creep up my cheeks.

"And before that?" He goes back to the desk kitty-corner to my bench, where he was sitting. He settles in and sips the scalding tea without as much as a wince.

"Miami."

He chuckles and shakes his head. "Miami. Hoo boy! No wonder you were unprepared."

"I guess so," I squash the urge to be defensive. If I had experience with snowstorms, I wouldn't have to be rescued.

"Well, Miss Miami, one thing at a time. Right now you have a smashed car, you're recovering from mild hypothermia, and the storm's still going strong out there. So the question is..." His eyes twinkle over the cup as he takes another swallow of tea. "What should I do with you in the meantime?"

His teasing tone sends a tingle through me, and only my shyness keeps me from smiling.

Maybe it's from nearly dying, maybe it's him saving my life—or maybe it's because he's a big, competent, brave, seemingly gentle man with a voice like melted chocolate. The more I talk to Carl, the more hot he becomes.

"Um," I manage, my cheeks burning. A dozen suggestions are on the tip of my tongue, but I can't shake any of them loose.

His eyes twinkle again, and he snickers with amusement, then takes another sip of his drink. "Drink your tea; you need to get your strength back."

I nod and pick up the cup, barely cooled, and sip at it as fast as I dare. I grow more alert as the cup drains. "Do you live up here alone?"

"Except for my animals, yeah." He finishes his tea and returns to the kettle on its trivet. "I'm quite self-sufficient here, not much need or want for guests."

"Am I intruding?" I ask worriedly.

"You're a special case." He glances at me as he pours. "First time in a long time I've had anyone up here, but you likely would have died otherwise. You were pretty chilled by the time I got you up here."

I nod and keep sipping the tea. I remember it vaguely: the numbness creeping up my limbs, pushing before it a leading edge of icy pain; my panic hardly receding even as he carried me up the mountain on his snowmobile telling me things would be all right.

"If you weren't out on the road..." I'm not gushing at him.

"You would have died."

His flat statement sends a shiver through me. He notices it and glances away, stirring his tea. "Sorry."

"It's true enough. More reason to be grateful to you." I finish my tea, and he takes it from me, refilling the mug and dropping in a bigger dollop of honey. I watch him, fascinated by those huge hands moving with such precision.

I wonder what they would feel like on me. "It... it's just tough to get used to the idea. I haven't been in many endurance situations."

"That's a bit obvious," he teases so gently that I relax a little. "Anyway, the danger's over, and you're staying here until the storm lets up. Then I'll give you a ride back to town."

"Thanks again." I watch him as I take my drink. "So...you never go into any of the cities around? The City, Poughkeepsie, Kingston?"

He scowls, like he tasted something bitter in his tea. "Not if I can help it. Big cities stopped appealing to me years ago."

"Oh." Awkward silence stretches as I try to figure out what to do with my hands. Maybe I should be nervous and distrustful? I'm alone on a mountainside in a stranger's home, a stranger that looks like he could break me in half.

Breathing the warm smells of tea and wood smoke and leather and cologne, I'm thinking about the other things that could happen between us—things far more fun than violence.

"So...are you planning to spend your holidays up here?" he asks. "You'll need some hand-holding if you wander through these woods in late December."

Here is an intensely private man telling me he never has guests, yet here he is showing an interest in me as well. He's making an offer. One I can really use.

"Are you offering to be the man who does it?" I ask quietly. "Because right now, after what you did, you're the only one I'd trust enough."

Running a hand through his hair, those feral-looking eyes sparkle with good humor. "If it will keep you from getting lost on the side of my mountain, yeah. I'll show you around. But only once you're settled."

I look around at his cozy place, its owner moving restlessly around it like a tiger in a cage. "You're bored, aren't you?"

He pauses...and then lets out a little laugh. "I suppose I am." He looks at me, and the twinkle in his eye becomes a gleam. "Besides, you're cute, and you're definitely *not* boring."

I give him a genuine smile. "All right, once I'm settled, I'll take you up on that offer."

CHAPTER 4

Carl

What the hell am I doing?
The storm ended as suddenly as it blew in; the wind slowed in minutes and the snow thinned down to nothing. Everything was blanketed in two feet of snow. After cute little Belle had some bread and goat cheese, I bundled her up and took her to town with her wardrobe in one of my spare duffel bags.

I'm doing post-storm damage control, trudging up and down the mountain in my snowshoes to check my wind turbines and wells and to wipe the snow off the solar panels. The livestock's fine; I checked them first. One of my sugar maples fell and took out part of my goat fence on the way down.

Before I let the herd out of their earth-sheltered barn, I need to make sure they can't go wondering off into the woods to become bear snacks. Cutting through the log and rolling it off the fence line takes time; so does repairing the breach.

The whole time, I'm thinking about Belle; it distracts me from the cold, the effort, the monotony. Makes my dick hard as hell, too, despite it being freezing.

Once I got the Bundle inside and set it on the heated bench next to the rocket stove and started unwrapping it, what I saw under all those clothes tempted me to keep unwrapping. Fortunately, I'm not an asshole—but the very sight and scent of her was enough to cause some wishful thinking.

How could any guy look at that adorable pixie and not want her? The silky blonde hair in its short French braid, her milky skin and curvy body, she's the most perfect-looking woman I've seen since I lost Elaine. Exactly my type—precisely!

Even if she has little common sense. Her baffled look when I told her this is my mountainside made me chuckle. Of course the Parks Department didn't tell her this was private land. People pass through here all the time without noticing much besides the wind turbines and their attendant shed, and I've never made a stink about it.

There's more to it, though. I try to keep things off the record, including my real name. There are many reasons to keep my name off the books—and my ass off-grid and out of sight.

Becoming a ghost in the system took me time and work, and I'm certain Everett doesn't believe I'm really dead. He and Cassidy have every reason to make sure I'm truly six feet under —just like Elaine. So staying out of sight is prudent.

Would Belle would be shocked to learn I'm actually from Chicago, and I masqueraded for years as a successful computer programmer to cover up my wealth? This land has been in my family for a very long time...but I wanted nothing to do with it until I had nowhere else to go. It's the last place my former partners would look for me, and thus the perfect place to hide.

Most of the time, anyway. It's not like people in town don't know me. But they don't know anything that could trace me back to my old life, and they don't know enough about me to do much besides spread baseless rumors—which makes the perfect smokescreen for a guy who would rather be known as an eccentric mountain man than a former bank robber on the run from his ex-partners.

I don't spend much time with others. Sometimes I clean myself up and go to the local ski lodge to pick up lonely women. We always go to their hotel; I never bring them home.

Some of them quickly started getting attached. It seems there's a shortage of good sex out here. It doesn't take much to make a woman obsess over you: some creativity, stamina, empathy, and a good knowledge of the female body.

I never see a woman more than a few times, I never date locals, and I definitely do not take them home.

Now though, I've got a problem. I brought a woman home...and she has occupied my thoughts ever since. I want her so badly I'm thinking of breaking my rules and spicing up our working arrangement.

With a lot of sex.

Once the fence is fixed, I check the livestock again, feed them, and gather eggs. Belle dances through my head, a constant, pleasant distraction. I make a Denver omelet on top of my rocket stove and lounge on the heated bench to eat it, catching faint traces of her perfume.

She's pretty naive...and very young. And nice as well as pretty. She won't suspect a thing if I am careful. I could still seduce her.

I pause with my fork halfway to my mouth and then smile lopsidedly. "Yeah. I could do that." The idea's very appealing.

The problem is, this attraction's so strong that I wonder if I could I let her go after? I might want to keep her. That would cause all kinds of complications.

Maybe it's time for a background check on this lady. She'll be around for a few months. That's long enough for her to find out things about me I don't want getting out.

If I find nothing, having a winter fling with Belle won't be such a risky prospect.

After washing up, I head for a built-in bookcase at the end of the hall. The front portion of my earthship home is small and cozy: a combination living room and kitchen, two bedrooms, one bathroom, and my workshop, all arranged along a single hallway. By removing two books from the shelf and switching them, however, the bookcase slides back and aside into a secure area beyond.

This is the real hearth of my home, where my wealth and my tech is hidden. Five more rooms are dug into the mountain and reinforced with concrete, stone, and steel. There's an aquaponic garden for vegetables, fruits, and fish, a machine room for the controls and house batteries, food and gear storage, a computer room in the rear, and an exit tunnel connected to the turbine shed.

The lights come turn on automatically as I step inside the cool, sterile room with its humming machines and whitewashed walls. Instead of windows, this and all the other completely underground rooms have flat-screens hung on the walls, each one showing views from the deer cams sprinkled across my property.

"Bach," I say distractedly and a violin concerto starts playing on the speaker. I cross the room and settle at the main workstation where three large screens sit at eye level.

"All right, little lady. Let's get to know you better."

It was my dick doing the talking when I offered to help her find photo opportunities on my mountainside. I could sit here and rationalize how keeping her close would make sure she doesn't take a picture of anything she shouldn't. But just how out of control was I?

It was an impulsive act, and recklessness is dangerous for a man in my position. Now, I need to know who I'm dealing with before we proceed.

I start a search on Belle Cantor and find her website, Facebook, and a few places where her work is being sold. She's actually a good photographer—and her focus is on animals, which is adorable.

Four photo books at twenty-four years old. One on pets, one on working animals, one on city wildlife, and on ferals in New York City. Some of the photos are fairly gritty, taking her into dark alleys in the parts of Hell's Kitchen that haven't been gentrified yet. Some of the neighborhoods are familiar; they remind me somewhat of home.

Scrolling through beautifully framed shot after shot, my mind drifts a bit and sends me back dozens of years to my young boyhood. Just me and my buddies, all those afternoons spent running and wrestling and playing games in the dappled sunlight of that tree-lined street.

Those were innocent and good times. Dad was still alive, working his ass off, while his sister Aunt Grace stayed with us after school. I was an ordinary kid with no clue of the kind of shit laying down life's road for me.

Belle's photographs capture sunlight, warmth, the freshness and the innocence, even when she's photographing a starving kitten rescued out of a Bronx alleyway. I drink them all in and remember, and it feels pretty good.

Then I review her personal information, and...out of the blue, what I'm looking at isn't as fun anymore. Maybe sweet little Belle isn't as naive and sheltered as I thought.

I force myself to read her online journal, though I quickly learn she uses the same password for everything. I'm not invading her privacy more than necessary to make sure she's safe to have around. I don't feel great about doing that at all.

Then again, it's for her safety as much as mine.

Any woman involved with me would become a target the moment my former partners find me. So even though it's creepy, I check the parts of her background that matter.

It's rather tragic. No registered father. Born in Miami, lived there until five years ago.

Moved to Poughkeepsie after accepting the first job she was offered... immediately after her mother married a guy named Blake Miller. Why does he sound familiar? I do a side search on him as I keep going through her things.

Medical records next. She's been perfectly healthy for most of her life. Track, swimming, hiking. But hiking in Florida is way different from hiking Upstate. She knows about dodging gators, but not the warning signs of a snowstorm.

No mention of a relationship; she wasn't wearing a ring, and her phone history didn't show any males she called regularly. In fact, there's nothing in her background that associates her with men at all. Maybe she doesn't date.

Maybe she's wary of men. Come to find out she has reason. Her stepfather, Blake Miller, is a piece of work. Arrested six times for assaulting women.

A single footnote in Belle's medical history pisses me off: hospitalization for a battering, and the very same night Blake Miller was arrested and charged for assault. He beat her!

He assailed her, and her mother stayed with him. Belle left and got as far from Miami as she could manage, worked in a photo lab for six months before her first two photo books became popular. And from what I can tell, she's never been home since.

Holy shit, that bastard. Poor Belle. And what is with her mom deciding the dude's more important? That's insane!

I push away from the computer, the wheels on my office

chair squeaking. "Okay. Enough being nosy. She's fucking clean."

Problem is, now I'm even more curious...and more fascinated.

If you want to continue reading this story, you can get your copy from your favorite vendor by searching for the title:

The Mountain Man's Secret

An Older Man Younger Woman Romance

You can also find the e-book version by typing this link in your computer's browser:

https://www.hotandsteamyromance.com/products/the-mountain-mans-secret-an-older-man-younger-woman-romance

OTHER BOOKS BY THIS AUTHOR

Saving Her Rescuer: A Billionaire & A Virgin Romance

I WAS JUST TRYING to get away from my crazy ex for the weekend when I ended up in a giant pileup on the highway up to Gore Mountain.

HTTPS://GENI.US/SAVINGHERRESCUER

~

SENSUAL SOUNDS: A Rockstar Ménage

LUST. Lies. Double lives.

. . .

THE ROCK and roll industry is full of people who are looking out for themselves and willing to do anything to rise to the top.

HTTPS://WWW.HOTANDSTEAMYROMANCE.COM/COLLECTIONS/
FRONTPAGE/PRODUCTS/SENSUAL-SOUNDS-A-ROCKSTAR-MENAGE

∽

ON THE RUN: A Secret Baby Romance

MURDER. Lies. Fraud. Just another day in the lives of billionaires and women on the run.

HTTPS://WWW.HOTANDSTEAMYROMANCE.COM/COLLECTIONS/
FRONTPAGE/PRODUCTS/ON-THE-RUN-A-SECRET-BABY-ROMANCE

∽

THE DIRTY DOCTOR'S TOUCH: A Billionaire Doctor Romance

I AM A MASTER. An elitist. I am at the top of my field, and I know what I am doing.

HTTPS://WWW.HOTANDSTEAMYROMANCE.COM/COLLECTIONS/
FRONTPAGE/PRODUCTS/THE-DIRTY-DOCTOR-S-TOUCH-A-
BILLIONAIRE-DOCTOR-ROMANCE

THE HERO SHE NEEDS: A Single Daddy Next Door Romance

HE'S the only man I've ever wanted...

HTTPS://WWW.HOTANDSTEAMYROMANCE.COM/COLLECTIONS/FRONTPAGE/PRODUCTS/THE-HERO-SHE-NEEDS-A-SINGLE-DADDY-NEXT-DOOR-ROMANCE

YOU CAN FIND all of my books here

HOT AND STEAMY Romance
https://www.hotandsteamyromance.com

ABOUT THE AUTHOR

Mrs. Love writes about smart, sexy women and the hot alpha billionaires who love them. She has found her own happily ever after with her dream husband and adorable 6 and 2 year old kids.
Currently, Michelle is hard at work on the next book in the series, and trying to stay off the Internet.
"Thank you for supporting an indie author. Anything you can do, whether it be writing a review, or even simply telling a fellow reader that you enjoyed this. Thanks

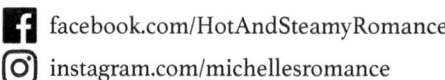 facebook.com/HotAndSteamyRomance
instagram.com/michellesromance

©Copyright 2020 by Michelle Love - All rights Reserved
In no way is it legal to reproduce, duplicate, or transmit any part of this document in either electronic means or in printed format. Recording of this publication is strictly prohibited and any storage of this document is not allowed unless with written permission from the publisher. All rights are reserved.
Respective authors own all copyrights not held by the publisher.

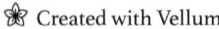 Created with Vellum